"Hello?
Oh, hi, Mom."

Clare had stepped out of the tub to answer the phone and was dripping soapy water all over the carpet. "What is it?"

A warm washcloth glided over her back, and she let out a startled exclamation. When she turned, Max was standing behind her with the cloth and a bucket full of warm water.

"Clare? Is anything wrong?"

"Ah, no, Mom. Go ahead." Clare tried to focus on her mother's story as Max sponged the soap from her body. But his ministrations felt too good to ignore.

"Well, dear," her mother went on, "Mrs. Bodiddle came in yesterday. . ." Max was now guiding the washcloth over her breasts and down her ribs, tickling her gently with each swipe.

"Anything else?" Clare asked, trying to keep the giggle from her voice. She turned to shoo Max away. He nodded as if responding to her silent suggestion—and let the towel drop from around his hips. The receiver slid from her nerveless fingers.

"Clare—? Clare—?"

Vicki Lewis Thompson, one of Harlequin Temptation's most popular authors, has already published ten Temptations. Her husband's experience in the insurance field helped her create this sexy and humorous story, which proves beyond doubt that insurance can be fun! Enhanced by the author's talent for characterization, *Full Coverage* is sure to make a delightful early-summer read.

HARLEQUIN TEMPTATION

HARLEQUIN SUPERROMANCE

Don't miss any of our special offers. Write to us at the following address for information on our newest releases.

Harlequin Reader Service
901 Fuhrmann Blvd., P.O. Box 1397, Buffalo, NY 14240
Canadian address: P.O. Box 603,
Fort Erie, Ont. L2A 5X3

Full Coverage
VICKI LEWIS THOMPSON

Harlequin Books

TORONTO • NEW YORK • LONDON
AMSTERDAM • PARIS • SYDNEY • HAMBURG
STOCKHOLM • ATHENS • TOKYO • MILAN

In appreciation to
Carol Albrecht Shutt,
for tips on saleswomanship,
and to Tom and Sylvia Sharpe,
for refreshing my memories
of the Gulf Coast.

FORTY YEARS OF
Romance

Published June 1989

ISBN 0-373-25356-7

1

MAX ARMSTRONG'S WINDOW, easily the size of a high-way billboard, reflected a picture-puzzle scene of snowy mountains and scudding clouds against a blue November sky. Clare watched with fascination as her orange golf ball approached the glass. When it hit, creating a jagged hole in the middle of the scene, she felt a moment of vandalistic joy. "Serves him right," she muttered before guilt took over and reminded her of the implications of her accident.

"Did I hear glass breaking?" Her seventeen-year-old brother leaped from the golf cart and jogged over toward her to get a better view. "Holy...uh, shucks. You broke Max Armstrong's window, Clare."

"Lord, I didn't mean to," Clare said, wondering if she had indeed meant to, unconsciously. "He'll come storming out any minute. This is not a good beginning, Joel."

"He won't come storming out, Clare. He's not home."

"Are you sure?" Clare glanced hopefully at her blond brother, so often mistaken for her twin despite their eleven-year age difference. "How can you tell?"

"No flag. He flies a teddy bear flag when he's home."

Clare looked at the empty flagpole at the corner of the deck and sighed with relief. "A teddy bear flag. It figures." She gazed across the shaved perfection of the green at the three-story structure that housed her business rival.

"Hey, the bears were a great idea. Admit it."

"So he has an effective gimmick. That doesn't make up for his complacency or lack of innovation."

"Maybe not," Joel said. "But you go into a house in Flagstaff and see one of those bears, and bam, you know Max Armstrong is their insurance agent. 'The Armstrong Teddy Bear, Symbol of Security.'"

"You don't have to remind me." Clare grimaced. "I hear that slogan in my sleep."

"Tom gave him the idea, though, when he was about six."

"Oh, yeah? I didn't know that." Clare studied the barn-gray structure. "Why does Max still live here, do you think? It's far too much house for one person."

"I think he keeps the house so Tom and Brian have something familiar to come back to when they visit their father," Joel said. He cocked his head to one side and looked at her. "So what are you going to do about the window?"

"Leave a note, I guess."

Joel pushed his tongue against the inside of his cheek and gazed at the clouds above them. "Wouldn't have to, you know. That golf ball doesn't have your name on it."

"Joel Pemberton! Are you suggesting that I sneak away and pretend I didn't do this?"

"Well, my moralistic big sister, have you considered the consequences? You're trying to beat Max out of insuring this resort, and he tells his client a great story about how you were the first golfer in history to break his window. Then they have a big laugh over it. Would that do you any good?"

Clare narrowed her eyes. "What do you mean, the first golfer in history? Max lives on a golf course. He must have broken windows all the time."

"Not according to Tom. He said it would take an incredibly bad golfer to come close to his windows, let alone hit a ball through them. In ten years he's only had a few balls land on the deck, and none through the windows. None, Sis."

"I'm really glad you shared that with me, Joel."

"Still going to leave a note? After all, I thought we played this round today so you could impress the resort owner with your knowledge of the game and his course." Joel glanced around. "Listen, nobody's coming up behind us. The course is practically deserted. We can go on to the eleventh tee and forget this."

Clare shook her head, determined to be honest for the benefit of her own conscience and as an example for her brother. After the death of their father she'd assumed a leadership position in the family and she took the responsibility seriously. "I'll leave my business card somewhere so he can see it," she said, handing Joel her five iron.

"How about tossing it through that big hole in his window? I imagine that will catch his attention, there among the shards."

"Thanks, Joel. Wonderful suggestion."

"I thought so."

"I'll be right back. Unless you want to walk up there with me?"

"No, thanks. Teenagers get enough bad press for breaking things. I'll keep my distance."

Clare climbed the gentle slope toward Armstrong's house. The area was meticulously landscaped with blue spruce and beds of white chrysanthemums. Several aspens, touched by frost, shivered in the wind like a fountain of gold coins. Red potted geraniums rimmed the large wooden deck and asparagus ferns draped from elaborate macramé hangers.

Clare mounted the stairs to the deck and fumbled in the pocket of her slacks for one of her business cards. She wrote her message with the stubby pencil she'd used for keeping her gargantuan score. "Sorry about the window. Let me know how you want this handled." She signed her initials and tossed the card through the jagged hole. Then she wished for it back, as if she'd mailed a letter and now realized that she didn't want it sent. But the card lay out of reach in the diamond-bright glass littering his gray carpet.

Figuring that she'd earned the right by owning up to her mistake, Clare decided to take a quick inventory of the teddy bear king's lair. A native rock fireplace covered an entire wall and another held a large oil painting of the Grand Canyon. A curved sectional in gray and brown plaid faced the fireplace and a baby grand piano with the cover up stood behind the sectional. At the end of the living room was a wet bar.

Joel must have loved coming over here, she thought, before the divorce had taken Tom and Brian to San Diego to live with their mother. No wonder Joel had wanted to emulate Max Armstrong instead of their far less successful father.

When she'd first considered going for this sale and knocking Max from his perch as the insurance agent for one of the biggest commercial policies in Flagstaff, Clare had calculated roughly what the annual premium would be. The amount had been enough to goad her on to further research. She'd discovered that Max had left himself vulnerable—he hadn't provided E.

Hamilton Durnberg with complete coverage for all the resort owner's needs. That would be her opening.

By taking the account away from Max she could tarnish his image a little in Joel's eyes and put the Pemberton Agency firmly in the black. It seemed a spectacular way to demonstrate to Joel that her financial training and computerized programs would pay off against Armstrong's more homespun methods and complacent methods of servicing his accounts. Two months ago Joel had announced that he planned to go straight into the agency and forget college, because money was tight and, besides, Max Armstrong had done quite well without a college education.

Clare had listened to Joel's announcement with growing alarm. She didn't know if Joel's future was in the insurance business or not, but if he failed to graduate from college first, he wouldn't leave himself many options. She wanted two things—money for Joel's education and a chance to prove that Max Armstrong could be beaten. Winning E. Hamilton Durnberg as a client would accomplish both goals.

ON MONDAY AFTERNOON Clare was rapidly feeding information into her computer in an attempt to finish up some paperwork before her appointment with Durnberg. The computer had been her first step in upgrading her father's office. She'd increased the revenue somewhat since she'd taken over the agency, enough to afford a part-time secretary or a computer. Clare had chosen the computer.

Consequently she depended on an answering machine when she left the office for an appointment. She'd tried to ignore the fact that she'd had no vacation in two years. With Durnberg as a client, all that would change, anyway.

When the front door opened Clare glanced up with impatience at the unwelcome interruption. Her irritation quickly turned to chagrin as she watched a tall man in a dark chocolate Western suit and a brown suede Stetson approach her desk. He was tossing an orange golf ball in the air.

Clare's face grew hot. She had no idea what to say to this self-assured man whose living room window she had destroyed. She'd expected a telephone call, perhaps from his secretary. She wasn't prepared for Max Armstrong in person, especially under such embarrassing circumstances.

"I'm—I'm sorry about your window," she said finally.

He tipped up the brim of his Stetson. His eyes were light brown, almost golden, and they glinted with amusement. "Two things amaze me about this incident," he said, placing the golf ball in the exact center of her desk where the green blotter held it in place.

Clare drew back in her chair, as if the golf ball might explode. "Two things?"

"First of all, I'd like to know how you managed what no other golfer has achieved before."

"Uh . . ." Clare stalled. "Freak shot, I guess."

"What club were you using?"

"It was, um, a five iron."

"From how far out?"

"Oh, maybe . . . maybe a hundred yards."

"Ye Gods, woman."

"It wasn't all my fault. The wind stopped."

"I wouldn't use a five iron to hit a hundred yards unless there was a hurricane blowing!"

"Joel said it might be too much club, but . . ." Clare paused to gather her scattered defenses. Deliberately moving the golf ball to the far side of her desk, she sat up straight and looked her antagonist in the eye. "I'll pay for the window, Mr. Armstrong. We really don't have to discuss how it happened, do we?"

He ignored her question. "So you know who I am?"

She cursed her slip in calling him by his name. Feigned ignorance of his identity would have served her better, but now she was obliged to feed his ego. "I've seen your picture in the newspaper."

"Not lately, I'm afraid. Say, do you mind if I sit down?"

"I do have an appointment at three, and I have some work to get out before—"

"I'll only be a minute," he said, relaxing into the chair opposite her desk as if he planned to stay the rest of the afternoon.

"I mean I have to be there at three, to—a sales call out of the office."

"Oh. Well, so do I, strangely enough. Your place was on my way, so I decided to stop in and satisfy my curiosity about you."

"My golf game needs a little work, Mr. Armstrong, if that's what you want to know."

"Max."

"All right, Max." She thought of Joel's warning that Max might turn this incident into a joke to amuse Durnberg. "Fortunately the knack of the game came back to me after the tenth hole. Even Joel commented at the end of the round that—"

"Joel. Is he your husband?"

"My brother." As soon as the words were out Clare berated herself for answering his questions so readily.

The easy tone of his voice prompted cooperation. He probably sold policies in just that tone of voice.

Max snapped his fingers. "That's right. Joel Pemberton. He's one of Tommy's friends."

"I believe they do know each other," Clare said, adopting Max's casual tone.

"And you're his older sister. Now it's coming back to me. Your father had this agency, and then he . . ."

"Died two years ago."

"Yes. I'm sorry. I didn't know him very well, but he seemed like a decent guy."

"He was."

"And you're running the agency these days?"

"Yes."

Max glanced around him. "I'll bet you've redecorated the office, too."

"What makes you think so?" She had, doing most of the work herself to save money, but she decided not to be so easy with the answers.

"Oh, I don't know." He shrugged. "The wall graphic looks freshly painted, and the pictures are something a young, bright, progressive woman would choose."

"What do you mean?" Clare couldn't decide if he liked the decor or not.

With his thumb Max tipped his Stetson to the back of his head. "Well, here's this red zig-zag line running around the wall looking like a sales chart—that's clever. And abstract art in chrome frames on the wall, which shows that you're progressive."

"I believe that's a good thing to be if you're an insurance agent."

"Oh, no doubt, no doubt." He leaned back in his chair.

"What pictures are on the wall in your office, Max?"

"A friend of mine dabbles in oils. He painted me a couple of nice landscapes, one of the peaks and another of the aspens in the fall. Folks seem to like looking at them." He folded his arms and smiled at her.

Clare didn't miss his almost deliberate use of the word *folks*. No, he didn't care for her decor, probably considered it cold and sterile. But whether he liked her office or not, Clare thought, he was looking at the future of the insurance business in Flagstaff. The day of winning people over with teddy bears was gone.

Max shifted in his seat but made no move to get up. "You look a lot like your brother. You're slender, like he is, and your hair's the same light blond, but I don't remember that his eyes were green."

"Joel's eyes are blue," Clare said automatically, used to the comparison with her brother. Everyone always remarked about the difference in eye color. "But I'm surprised you remember Joel that well."

"I always remember the good kids Tommy brought home. There were plenty of others who—well, never mind about that. Anyway, now that I know you're Joel's sister, I'm not the least surprised that you owned up to this accident. But that was the second thing that amazed me. The person who broke that window didn't have to admit it—you did."

Clare fought against the welcome feeling of his praise after his implied disapproval of her office. Damn it, she shouldn't care what this guy thought about her office, her brother or her ethics. But the nature of his charisma made neutrality difficult.

She guessed his age at forty-one or forty-two. He'd reached the time of life when some men began to look more attractive and others more tired. Max belonged to the first group. He held his shoulders back, his head up, in the posture of authority that sometimes accompanied financial success. Clare could understand why Joel admired Max's personal style, just from the brief time she'd spent with him today.

The power of his personality was considerable. He'd engaged her in conversation and made her forget the work in her computer which now wouldn't be finished before her appointment. She glanced at her watch. "I'll have to leave soon, Max. What will the window cost to replace? I may decide to file a claim on my—"

"Forget it."

"What?"

"The window's replaced. The glass people came out right away, and I put in the claim on my policy. Don't worry about it."

"But I'm sure you have a deductible, and I—"

"Didn't cost me anything. I've sent enough business to the glass company over the years that they didn't mind waving the deductible. In fact, they wanted to do the whole thing for free, but I drew the line at that. Everyone has to make a living."

Clare had the uncomfortable feeling of being in his debt. "I haven't made any sort of restitution, and I want to."

Max chuckled. "You *do* have a guilty conscience, don't you? Want to buy me a drink sometime?"

The suggestion gave her an unexpected jolt and she realized that her palms were sweating. "Well, I—"

"Hey, never mind. You probably have a steady guy who wouldn't go for that."

"No, but—"

"No? Then I'll make the invitation definite. Let's get together for a drink. My three-o'clock appointment may tie me up for the rest of today, but how about if I pick you up at five tomorrow afternoon?"

Heart pounding, Clare fumbled for an excuse, but she'd always been terrible at fibs. Besides, by tomorrow afternoon Max would know she was after his resort account and he would probably cancel their date for drinks. "All right," she said, in a voice that didn't sound like hers.

"Great. I'll look forward to it." He stood up and held out his hand.

After a moment's hesitation Clare also stood and placed her hand in his. The warmth of his fingers came as a second shock to her system. Had she expected him to be cold-blooded, literally and figuratively? Instead the firm pressure of his hand sent alarming sensations racing through her. She couldn't remember a man's touch ever having such a volatile effect, and she was frightened.

"Hey, I invited you for a drink, not a public lynching," he said softly.

"Sorry." She smiled self-consciously and wondered what he must think of her behavior.

"Same dimples."

"What?"

"You and Joel. Same dimples. Say hello to him for me, will you?"

Clare gulped. "Sure." What was happening to her? She had to remain calm with this man. He was her rival, whether he knew it or not, and she needed to keep a cool head.

"Until tomorrow, then." Max released her hand.

"Right." When he was no longer touching her, Clare felt the shakes take over. She placed both palms on the firm surface of the desk and leaned against it as she watched Max Armstrong walk to the front door of her office.

He paused in the clients' waiting area, beside the magazine table. "Anybody read these?" he asked, picking up issues of *Forbes* and *Money*.

"I do."

"I mean your clients."

"I—I don't know. My theory is that they need to be informed about the current financial climate, so I have magazines and pamphlets there that will help."

"Whew," Max said and replaced the magazines in the same linear arrangement in which he'd found them.

"I take it you don't have such magazines in your waiting area?"

"Nope."

Clare couldn't resist asking. "What, then?"

"Oh, you know. *Readers' Digest, Time, People*. Stuff I like to read."

"It just so happens that I like to read *Forbes* and *Money*," Clare replied.

He nodded and glanced at the abstract watercolor on the wall near the door. "I'll bet you do, at that." Then, before she could respond, he touched the brim of his hat in a gallant gesture of farewell and was gone.

Of all the stupid things in the world to happen, she mused as he walked away from her glass-fronted office. Why hadn't he just called? Now she was dealing with a real man. The phrase stuck in her mind. *A real man*. Those words, with all of their implications, hit her like an avalanche. No, she thought, she would not give room to a single such thought about Max Armstrong. She couldn't afford to.

Exiting her program on the computer and protecting the terminal and keyboard with a dust cover, Clare picked up the file containing her presentation for Durnberg and tucked it into the briefcase her mother had given her last Christmas. Her mother had overspent in gratitude for Clare's willingness to run the agency and keep her out of the poorhouse. Clare doubted that Max Armstrong had a more elegant briefcase than hers.

She mustn't think of Max, she chided herself as she turned on the answering machine and locked the office. This meeting with Durnberg demanded all her concentration if she expected to take business away from the most successful agent in Flagstaff.

As she drove her ten-year-old Datsun through the pillared entrance to Flagstaff Fairways Resort, Clare noticed that hers was the oldest vehicle on the road or in the driveways of the spacious homes she passed on her way to the clubhouse. Joel had often declared that someday he'd have a Porsche like Max Armstrong. She was impatient with her brother's fixation on expensive cars, yet at this moment she wouldn't have minded sitting behind the wheel of something a little newer, a little shinier.

Her father had never seemed to mind presenting a shabby exterior. At times she'd suspected that he wore poverty as a badge of honor. Clare had attempted to cultivate the same attitude toward material possessions, but she'd never quite gotten the knack of it, although she still tried. Joel refused to try at all, and that worried her tremendously.

The Flagstaff Fairways clubhouse sprawled amidst a stand of giant ponderosa pines that kept the grounds crew busy sweeping up pine needles from the sidewalks and picking pine cones out of the flower beds.

The trees had been preserved to keep the mountain resort atmosphere around the clubhouse, but Clare hated to imagine how many of the huge trees had been sacrificed to the design of the golf course. The new condominium and time-share units also required drastic recontouring of the land, but all this, she kept reminding herself, contributed to the value of the resort and added to the insurance premium. The premium's renewal was in exactly two months, on January fifteenth. Clare wanted Durnberg to have plenty of time to consider her proposal before then.

She parked her car and walked toward the massive wooden doors of the main entrance. She already knew that a fire hydrant sat to the right of the building, and that there were plenty of hydrants spaced along the winding roads in front of the condo and time-share units. Fire was a major concern of insurance companies working in Flagstaff, and she didn't want this deal to fall through for lack of proper fire protection.

She paused outside the double doors to take a deep breath. She'd prepared for this appointment for weeks, researching the needs of the resort and matching them with an insurance package that carried an attractively low price tag. But she knew Max couldn't be beaten on price alone, so she had added a plan for Durnberg's other resort in Florida, Sugar Sands, and a health and life insurance package. She would sell her program as inclusive, one-stop shopping, with all of Durnberg's insurance needs handled by a single agent—her.

Logically all she had to do was present her plan to win the business away from Max, yet she wouldn't allow herself to believe that everything would be that easy. Max had been the Flagstaff Fairways agent for a

long time. She might have to fight both loyalty and in-
ertia, but she was determined to overcome either or
both. Squaring her shoulders, Clare pulled open the
heavy door.

She'd walked through the carpeted lobby before,
knew where Durnberg's office was located. That had
been part of her original scouting trips before Durnberg arrived in town. He only spent brief periods at the
resort, preferring the gentler climate of Sugar Sands on
the Gulf of Mexico at Longboat Key.

The receptionist at the front desk smiled at Clare but
seemed nervous. "Durnberg told me to send you right
in," she said, glancing back toward the half-open office door. Then she lowered her voice. "And good luck."

"Thanks, Beverly." Clare had become friends with
the receptionist and through her had learned a great
deal about both resorts. If Clare got the account, she
planned to take Beverly out for a steak dinner.

And she would get the account, she promised herself as she walked down the short hall to Durnberg's
office. The sound of two male voices made her pause
for a moment. Damn, she'd wanted to have Durnberg
to herself, yet he must have some resort employee with
him. Perhaps the employee was about to leave.

In spite of Beverly's statement that she could walk
right into the office, Clare tapped lightly on the partially open door. She could see neither Durnberg nor
his visitor, who were both on the far right side of the
office, hidden by the door.

"Come in," called a man, presumably Durnberg.

Clare stepped through the doorway with an expec-
tant smile for the man sitting behind the desk. Then,

forgetting her manners entirely, she stopped to stare openly at the other person in the room.

He turned in his chair and touched the brim of his Stetson. "Nice to see you again so soon, Clare."

2

"SO YOU'VE MET, THEN." The slim man behind the desk smiled, revealing orthodontically perfect teeth.

"Yes. Just this afternoon." Clare gave her attention with difficulty to the person she had come to see. The gray at his temples and his fine-boned face suggested aristocracy, a familiarity with money and privilege. Whereas Max looked as if he'd be comfortable with a beer in his hand at a neighborhood bar, this man did not.

The office was paneled in a rough-hewn wood that suited Max more than this carefully polished man. The furniture consisted of a heavy desk with two uphol-stered chairs arranged in front of it, a leather loveseat against one wall, and a glass trophy case against the other. The case was full of golf and tennis trophies that belonged, Clare assumed, to Durnberg. On top of it sat a teddy bear.

"Perhaps I misunderstood the appointment time, Mr. Durnberg," Clare said. "I'll be glad to come back later, after you've had a chance to—"

"No, no. I planned this. Come, sit down next to my good friend Max."

Clare winced. So Durnberg considered Max his friend. "Actually, if you don't mind, Mr. Durnberg, I'd rather—"

"Listen, Ham, I don't think the young lady is happy with this arrangement." Max rose from his chair. "I can leave for a little while, take a walk or something."

Clare's eyes widened. Was Max that generous, that he'd quit the field and allow her room to operate? More likely he didn't consider her a threat. After all, he'd called this fellow "Ham," against her formal-sounding "Mr. Durnberg."

"I don't want either of you to leave," Durnberg said firmly. "There's been a change in my plans and I decided the simplest way to handle this would be talking to both of you at once."

Clare tightened her grip on her briefcase. "What change of plans?"

"Have a seat, Ms Pemberton, and I'll tell you."

Clare moved gingerly toward the chair next to Max and sat on the edge of the seat.

Durnberg looked at both of them with an amused expression. "What did you do to her at this meeting you had this afternoon, Max? She acts frightened to death of you."

Max leaned back in his chair and crossed one foot over the knee closest to Clare. She was surprised to notice that the sole of his polished boot was quite worn.

His smile was easy as he looked at Durnberg. "Maybe she thinks I'll be mad because she's here trying to take business away from me."

Clare stiffened at his nonchalance, which told her clearly that he didn't fear her intrusion at all. "I assume you think that's impossible?"

Max chuckled and glanced at her. "Anything's possible, but life's too short to get worked into a lather about a little competition."

She opened her mouth to challenge his evaluation of "a little competition," but Durnberg interrupted.

"Friendly competition, that's what I like to see. And along those lines, I have a proposition for you two. I've been called back to Florida immediately. Some personnel problems demand my attention and I'm flying out of Flagstaff early tomorrow morning. I also have a few things to clear up here before I leave, which doesn't allow me time to consider Ms Pemberton's proposal and compare it with your coverage, Max. I suggest you both come with me to Florida."

Clare gasped. "Well, I—"

"I'd love it, Ham," Max said quickly.

Clare tried to calm her racing pulse. Max was going. If she stayed behind, she'd never get this account. Besides, going to Florida would play right into her hand. "How long are we talking about?"

"Just a few days," Durnberg said, already glancing through some papers on his desk as if the issue were settled. "I'm sure both of you can leave your agencies with your secretaries for that small amount of time."

"Gloria wouldn't mind doing without my ugly mug for longer than that. I think she considers me a nuisance," Max said.

Clare thought quickly. She had no choice but to go, yet who would handle everything in her absence? "I'll— I'll make the necessary arrangements," she murmured.

"Good." Durnberg glanced up. "I'll see you both at the airport by six, if that's not too early for you?"

"Not at all," Max said, rising from the chair. "I can use some time in the sun to work on my tan. Make sure it's shining while we're there, will you, Ham?"

"Max, the sun always shines on E. Hamilton Durnberg. You should know that by now." Durnberg smiled.

"Then I'll just stick next to you and catch the reflected glow."

"You do that, Max. See you in the morning, Ms—say, can we drop the formalities, Clare?"

"Certainly, Mr. Durnberg."

"No, it's *Ham*. Get Max to tell you the story behind that one. But don't tell her all the stories, Max. I have to preserve some dignity. Now run along, both of you."

Clare hadn't been told to run along since she was five, and that, coupled with Durnberg's obvious ego problem grated on her nerves. Just her luck that Durnberg would be tough to like.

When Max allowed her to precede him out of the office, she mumbled her thanks and hurried down the hall in hopes that she'd ditch him. His footsteps immediately behind her ended such hopes.

Soon he was walking beside her. "Seems like I have extra time this afternoon after all. How about that drink?"

Clare stopped and glanced up at him. "Now?"

"Why not?"

"If I'm leaving tomorrow, I have several things to take care of," she hedged.

"So do I, but let's have that drink, anyway."

She searched his expression for ulterior motives. "I'm very serious about winning this account away from you, Max. You can't buy me a drink and charm me out of it."

"I thought you were the one buying."

"Oh. Well, I suppose I did agree . . ."

"Come on." He took her elbow. "Let's not debate this. I'd like to sit and relax for a few minutes and you look as if you could use a break, yourself."

"Okay." His touch rattled her enough to weaken further protests. "I take it you know where we're going."

"Right down the hall. This place has a nice bar. Looks out on the eighteenth green."

"I know."

Max chuckled. "Maybe I should ask you if the windows are all intact, considering you passed this way yesterday."

"That wasn't funny."

"No, it wasn't. Sorry."

His apology surprised her. She had trouble taking the measure of this man striding purposefully beside her. She decided to probe the depth of his compassion. "Max, I have no right to ask this, but I'd really appreciate it if you wouldn't tell Durnberg about my little accident."

"I won't."

"Really?"

"Of course not." He guided her through the door of the cocktail lounge.

"That's very nice of you."

"Maybe, but it's smart business sense, too. I've never found any sales advantage to running down the competition. The client thinks you're full of sour grapes, or maybe even a liar. Unless I know for a fact that an agent or a company is crooked and I fear for the welfare of my client, I have nothing but good things to say about other salespeople and other companies." He chose a secluded booth in the corner and helped her into it before sliding in next to her. "And I know you're not dishonest. You've proven that already."

Clare edged a few more inches away from him on the leather seat. She was far too aware of his body, of the rhythm of his breathing and the flick of his eyelashes as he glanced at her. She swallowed and folded her hands on the table. "I appreciate your attitude."

"Good. Not everyone does. What would you like to drink?"

"White wine. The house brand will be fine."

He said nothing, but when the waiter appeared Max ordered Jack Daniel's on the rocks for himself and a premium Chardonnay for Clare.

The gesture made her feel more secure in her estimation of Max. This was the man she'd expected all along, someone with a bulldozer's approach to life who wouldn't hesitate to make arbitrary decisions for others. She decided to accept the extra expense rather than insist on a cheaper drink. This particular skirmish didn't matter.

"You know," she began, settling into the booth to gaze at him, "I'm interested in your theory about speaking well of your competition. It reminds me of the advice Thumper's father gave. But you probably didn't see *Bambi*."

"Oh, yes I did. Read it, too. And the quote is: 'If you can't say something nice about someone, don't say anything at all.'"

Clare laughed in surprise. "I wouldn't have expected you to be a *Bambi* fan."

In the shadowed booth his eyes had become a deeper brown. He leaned his forearms on the table. "Who do you think I am, the great white hunter who shoots Bambi's mother?"

"Maybe not that brutal, but I can picture you stalking Bambi's father."

He tipped his hat back with his thumb. "Can you really?"

"Well, look at the way you dress. You're right out of the pages of a Western-wear catalogue, just before the section on guns."

"Then you won't mind if I chew a little tobacco while we sit here? I promise not to spit in your direction." He reached into his coat pocket.

"I most certainly would mind! I think chewing tobacco is a terrible habit. Don't you know that it promotes lip and gum cancer? And as for the practice of spitting, why, I have never—" She stopped her harangue when the waiter brought their drinks. Then as she noticed Max's amusement for the first time, she realized that he'd been kidding her. "You don't really chew."

"No," he said with a grin, removing his hand from his pocket.

Clare admitted to herself that she preferred Max's smile to Durnberg's. Durnberg reminded her of a toothpaste ad, and his expressions seemed carefully calculated. Max's reaction to her was spontaneous, and she responded with a sheepish smile of her own. "You really pushed my button on that one."

"So I noticed."

Heat warmed her cheeks. "I've given that speech to Joel several times. He plays baseball, and for a while he thought chewing tobacco was a requirement of the game. Besides, if he thought you used it..." She caught herself but it was too late.

"Why would I have anything to do with whether he chewed or not?"

"Well, any adult he came in contact with would be some influence."

"Granted, but he was at the house a maximum of three times, I'd say. Or is there something you're not telling me?"

Clare focused on her wineglass. "Sometimes adults have no idea how much they shape impressionable lives, even if the contact is brief."

"Hmm."

She glanced up to see if he was buying her evasion. Judging from his expression, he wasn't.

Nevertheless he shrugged and picked up his glass, as if willing to drop the subject of impressionable Joel. "Here's to friendly competition."

"To friendly competition," Clare repeated, although she couldn't imagine how she and Max could be friends after one of them became the victor in this contest. She touched the rim of her glass to his and glanced into his eyes.

Big mistake, she thought immediately and looked away again. Gentle humor and good will shone from those eyes, and something else, something that made her hands tremble and her heart beat a little faster as she sipped her drink. Damn, she was really and truly attracted to him. Damn. "Nice wine," she mumbled and took another sip.

"I can't see any point in drinking the cheap stuff. And this will be on me, considering I ordered it for you."

"Don't be silly. I can afford the extra money." *But I can't afford to like you, so stop being so likable.*

"I know how it is when you're working to build up an agency. You count every penny. Don't worry about this trip, though. When Durnberg treats, he really treats. You'll have a luxurious stay."

"I'm not there for luxury. I'm there to do business."

Max smiled at her over the rim of his glass. "You'd better act as if you're having fun, though, if you want to make Durnberg happy."

She gazed at him. "Why are you giving me tips on how to handle Durnberg?"

"Damned if I know," he said cheerfully.

"I do. You don't think I stand a chance."

"Oh, I wouldn't be stupid enough to think that, but I will admit your chances are slim."

"How long have you known him?"

"Durnberg? We went to high school together."

Clare felt like using one of Joel's favorite colorful expressions. The cards were stacked against her even more than she had thought. "I see."

"But we didn't run in the same crowd."

She found little comfort in his statement. "But you know how he came to be called 'Ham.'"

"Sure. He was in drama all four years and starred in most of the plays. With a middle name like Hamilton, his nickname was a natural."

Clare nodded. Durnberg's background explained his studied mannerisms. She'd known a few high school and college actors who had lost the distinction between role-playing and real life. Durnberg was obviously one of those people.

She glanced at Max. "So he was in the drama crowd, and you were a jock," she guessed.

"You really think you have me pegged, don't you?"

"Am I right?"

"In this case you are. But be careful about putting me in a slot, Clare. I won't fit."

"I'm beginning to understand that already."

"Good." He leaned back against the booth. "Correct me if I'm wrong, but aren't you operating a one-woman office?"

"What do you mean?"

"I didn't see a secretary around when I paid you a visit this afternoon. There wasn't even a desk for one."

"You're right. There's no secretary. I have a computer instead."

"That thing didn't look complicated enough to handle the office if you're in Florida."

"No," Clare admitted. "My, uh, mother can fill in for me while I'm gone." Clare shuddered inwardly at the thought but couldn't come up with any other solution. She'd been trying to solve the dilemma of her empty office ever since Durnberg proposed the trip, and her mother was the only answer on such short notice. God help the Pemberton Insurance Agency.

"She's done that for you before?"

"Yes." Clare tried not to think about the one other time her mother had taken over, when Clare had come down with the flu. Erasing all the computer programs wasn't even the worst of it. In two days Edna Pemberton had created a tangle of mistakes that had taken Clare two weeks to unravel.

"You're lucky to have someone with experience. I'll have trouble surviving when Gloria leaves me. She's a licensed agent herself now with plans to open her own agency eventually. Then I'll lose her help and gain a competitor. Fortunately I should be safe for a few more months, yet."

That's what you think, Clare mused to herself. "But isn't that a little disloyal of her?" she said aloud. "I'm sure she'll use the training she's received working for you."

"Of course she will. And I've encouraged her all the way. She's too bright to continue working for someone else all her life, although at first she balked at that idea."

"You encouraged her?"

"Why not?"

"Because in the end she might hurt your business."

"I can't operate under that premise, Clare. I figure you do the right thing by people. The business will take care of itself."

Clare felt warm words of agreement springing to her lips and realized she was really starting to like this man. That could seriously mess up her plans. She spoke quickly, determined to change her response to him. "Are you always this full of platitudes or are you trying to impress me with what a wonderful guy you are?"

He regarded her with surprise and something more. He was hurt.

"My God, that sounded terrible," she said, flushing. "Excuse my bad manners."

"You're excused," he said mildly. "And to answer your question, I'm trying to impress you, of course. Underneath I'm really a slimy scum bucket, but I'm hoping you won't discover that until it's too late."

"Too late for what?"

Max sighed. "Is there some reason you want to think of me as the one with the black hat?"

"Of course not. It's just—"

"Because you're behaving as if this is a war, where you have to believe the enemy is subhuman in order to shoot him. What we have here is the free enterprise system. Sometimes you have to mow down some real princes, because if you don't, they'll get the account and you'll be on the corner with a tin cup. There's nothing personal in it."

She glared at him. "Was my father one of the princes you mowed down?"

"I hope not, but from the tone of your voice I'd say you think so. I didn't know him very well."

She was stung by his lack of knowledge of her father, when her father had considered Max Armstrong his public enemy number one. Apparently Max had not even been aware of that fact. It had been a war from the vantage point of the Pemberton household, but obviously a one-sided war.

She stared at Max wordlessly for a moment. The longer she stayed alone in his company, the greater her chances of confusing her priorities. She consulted her watch with a show of alarm. "Heavens, it's getting late and I have a million and one things to do before we leave in the morning. I'd really better be going."

Max stood when she did. "Certainly. And don't worry about the tab. You can buy the next round."

Clare's smile was frosty. "Round two? This sounds like a fight, after all."

Max shook his head. "It doesn't have to be."

"I'm afraid you're wrong. And I'll warn you fair and square that I intend to win this bout. The Flagstaff Fairways account will belong to the Pemberton Agency very soon."

"You're a very determined young woman."

She nursed her anger, allowed it to show a little. "You say that as if you were speaking to a child. I'm not a child, Max."

"Oh, I'm well aware that you're not." His glance flicked over her. "Maybe I should warn you of something, too. Ham Durnberg is a consummate game player."

"I know that. Tennis, golf, racquet—"

"I don't mean organized games, although he loves those, too. I mean people games."

"So?"

"Think about why he's inviting us to Florida together."

"Because it's the most convenient way for him to compare our programs."

"Maybe."

She considered his veiled implications. "It doesn't matter what he's up to," she said finally. "I have the best insurance program, and he's a shrewd businessman. That's all that is important."

"Then I'll see you in the morning, Clare Pemberton."

"You surely will, Max Armstrong. And thank you for the drink." She turned and left the bar, aware of the movement of each muscle in her body as she walked away under his scrutiny.

Max kept his appreciative gaze on her gently swaying backside until it disappeared from sight. She was tall, at least five-eight, and a good portion of that was long, gorgeous legs. One of his secret passions was tall women who carried themselves well. Clare certainly qualified.

Once she was gone Max picked up his drink and finished it. Jack Daniel's was too expensive to waste, as he'd become painfully aware in the past few months. Fortunately beginning tomorrow he'd be drinking Ham's booze for a while, what little of it he consumed, anyway. Beginning tomorrow he'd also be thrown into a whirlwind of activities—golf, tennis, Windsurfing races, all competitive sports that Ham had spent hours in training for.

Ham loved to beat anyone at anything, but Max knew that Ham particularly liked to beat Max Armstrong. That was okay with Max, as long as Ham continued to put money in the till. But what exactly did he have in mind with this little Florida caper?

The only thing Max could figure was that Ham wanted to put his longtime agent and sometime friend through his paces, make him work for his commission a little. The fact that his competition came packaged as a beautiful blonde probably delighted Ham. He could watch Max struggle to keep from alienating the woman while he took business out from under her lovely nose.

Max wasn't sure how he could do that juggling trick, either. He'd like to manage it, though, he decided as he swigged the last of the Jack. Clare intrigued him more than any woman he'd encountered since his divorce, but his main concern was keeping the Fairways account. If he could do that and pursue Clare Pemberton, so much the better.

He couldn't believe that Ham had invited Clare because he was seriously considering a change in agents. He'd relished having Max at his beck and call for too many years to give up that ego trip. No, Ham was just playing one of his games, something to keep himself amused. Max felt a little sorry for Clare, but not sorry enough to toss her the business. With what Adele was putting him through, he couldn't afford to be that generous.

After signaling the waiter and paying for the drinks, Max left the cocktail lounge. He calculated that by driving quickly he'd catch Gloria before she left for the day. He would hate to bother her at home with the details of tomorrow's trip, considering she'd been married less than a month. He thought again about how her marriage had surprised everyone who had assumed Max's divorce occurred because he was fooling around with his secretary. He shook his head. If they only knew.

The Porsche started reluctantly. It needed a tune-up and a new set of tires, both of which would have to wait. As he drove toward his office Max tried to remember if he'd had any of his summer jackets and slacks cleaned since the weather turned colder and if his bathing suit was in good enough shape to take.

Then he wondered if he was in good enough shape himself to appear in a bathing suit. He'd always assumed his physique was adequate until the California surfer type had arrived and made off with his wife. Then here came his chance to go to Florida with a blonde who walked around in a less-than-thirty-year-old body. And damn it, he didn't want her to think of him as an old man on this trip. Max wanted... Oh, hell, what he wanted was for someone young and gorgeous to fall madly in love with him as they lay together on the pearly sands of the Florida Gulf Coast.

He had to admit there were a few problems with that image. Clare was young and gorgeous enough, but her mind was focused on business—his business, to be exact. When she didn't get it, she'd be an unlikely candidate for romance.

Max sighed and turned into his assigned parking space. At the rate Adele was going he wouldn't be able to afford this office much longer, no matter how much he enjoyed the renovated stone building in the heart of downtown. Soon he might be back to a little cubbyhole in a strip shopping center—a match for Clare Pemberton's office minus the wall graphic and the computer.

Clare was the new breed, he guessed. He didn't relate to her style of doing business, but he sure enjoyed looking at her. It would be a shame if they never got beyond this crazy Durnberg matter so they could become better acquainted. She was obviously smart as a whip and honest, both qualities he treasured.

He'd always remember the inviting picture she'd made when he first walked toward her office. The overhead lights had made her blond hair glow as she bent over her work. The shining strands hung forward like gold lamé, shadowing her face until the moment she looked up and he gazed into the green of her eyes. At that moment he'd been very glad that her golf ball had sailed through his window.

Max walked in the door to his office at five minutes past five to find Gloria still there typing a homeowner's policy that needed to be finished for an early-morning closing on a house.

She glanced up with a smile. "How's Ham Durnberg these days?"

"Up to his old tricks." Max wasn't surprised that people had linked him with this red-haired beauty. But the chemistry hadn't been there between them, not even when he'd been divorced and become available. Instead of lovers they had become very good friends. "Whenever you have to stay late to type something I feel guilty because I haven't bought you a computer."

"You're not the computer type, Max. I know that."

"Yeah, but I understand they speed up this sort of thing you're doing now."

She glanced at him. "Look, if you were rolling in clover I might start pressuring you about the computer again, but you can't afford one right now, so forget it. The typewriter works fine."

"Why not let me finish it up so you can go home to your hubby?"

"I'm nearly done. And hubby will understand."

"I hope he'll understand when he finds out you'll be holding the fort for the next few days. Durnberg's summoned me to Florida."

Gloria stopped typing. "Again? Listen, while you're there why don't you check into getting licensed in Florida so you can also cover the Sugar Sands Resort?"

"Aw, I hate to start that, Gloria. Then I'd have to find an agent who could help service the account, and Durnberg would probably drag me off there even more often."

Gloria rubbed her fingers together. "More money, Max."

"I know. And I could use it, but Durnberg's such a pain as it is. Besides, he might not want to give me Sugar Sands. He can't have me becoming too prosperous."

"We're not in danger of that," Gloria said with a wry grin.

Max sat on the edge of Gloria's desk and took off his Stetson. "Tell that to Adele. Anyway, Durnberg's trying to make me believe I've got some competition for the Fairways account." He pinched the crown of the Stetson between his thumb and forefinger. "A gal named Clare Pemberton has a program to show him that's supposed to be better than ours. He's dragging us down to Florida with him so he can consider both options at his leisure."

"Sounds like typical Durnberg manipulation. Is she pretty?"

"Yeah."

"The plot thickens." Gloria tapped her lips with one finger. "Pemberton. Isn't that Bill Pemberton's daughter? You know, the agent who died of cancer a couple of years ago?"

"That's her. She's running the business all by herself these days, although I guess her mother helps out now and then."

"Bill Pemberton was always a small-time agent, as I recall, but his daughter must be cut of a different cloth if she's going after the Fairways account."

"She won't get it."

"Oh, I'm sure she won't. But knowing Ham, he'll make her think she will, and maybe even put some doubts in your mind, too."

"Just so long as it's only a game. I can't afford to play for keeps on this one."

Gloria reached out and patted his arm. "Don't worry. You've had that account for ten years. Ham wouldn't know what to do without having you catering to him."

"Maybe he'd rather have a pretty young thing like Clare do the catering."

"Do you think so?"

Max shook his head. "Not really. I watched him this afternoon. He staged a cute little triangular meeting with the three of us to explain the situation."

Gloria made a face.

"Yeah, and Clare had no idea what she was walking into, poor kid. Anyway, I've been around Ham enough to know whether or not he's interested in a woman, and he showed no signs of going after this one."

"How about you?"

"Me? Hey, she's just a kid," Max said, unwilling to reveal his juvenile-sounding fantasies about Clare.

"Less than thirty, for sure. Hell, her brother is one of Tommy's friends."

Gloria arched copper-colored eyebrows. "What's that got to do with anything? I repeat my question."

"Your question is academic. Even if I were interested, such things are a two-way street. I can't imagine what she'd want with me, especially after she loses out on this account."

"You can't imagine? Max, your ego is in worse shape than I thought."

He nodded and stood up. "Ain't that the truth.... Well, you'd better finish that policy while I take inventory of what needs to be done while I'm gone."

"Right, boss."

"Sometimes I wonder if that's what I am. Lately you've been the driving force around here."

"You're in a little slump, that's all. Divorce can do that, especially an expensive one."

"Yeah." Max turned toward his desk. Then he paused and gazed at the shelves of teddy bears lining one wall of the office. "Gloria, do you know that saying by Thumper's father?"

"Who?"

"It's a rabbit, a character in *Bambi*."

"Sorry boss, but I've never been much for Disney movies."

"Oh." Max wondered if that was part of the underlying reasons why he and Gloria hadn't become an item. Come to think of it, Adele hadn't been much into Disney flicks, either. He'd been the one who had taken the boys to the movies to see the fairy-tale classics.

Max would lay money that Clare had seen them all and had loved them. She'd probably also read every single book by A.A. Milne, although he doubted that was true of his secretary. He decided to test that theory. "Say, Gloria, have you ever read *Winnie-the-Pooh*?"

"Whatever I know about stuffed bears I've learned in this office." Gloria swiveled her chair to study him with curiosity. "What gives with the twenty questions?"

"Nothing." Max thought some more. "Do you think I'm full of platitudes?" he said at last.

Gloria burst out laughing. "I think you're full of something, all right, and it's not platitudes."

"Thanks."

"You're welcome. Who told you that you were full of platitudes?"

"A blonde."

"By the name of Clare Pemberton?"

"Could be."

Gloria pursed her lips and cocked her head to one side.

"What are you looking at me like that for?"

"Max Armstrong, you have all the signs of a crush."

"Great. Just what I wanted to hear."

"Want my advice?"

"No."

"I'll give it to you anyway. Go get her, Max."

3

CLARE DROVE STRAIGHT from Flagstaff Fairways to her mother's house. Without her help, there would be no trip to Florida, and she had to go. The final motivation was Max's attitude. He didn't expect her to take this account away from him. He'd even implied that Durnberg was toying with her, pitting her against Max the Lion for Durnberg's amusement. She'd show him. She'd show them all.

Her mother lived in the same little house on Humphreys Street that Clare had grown up in. The contrast between the small two-story house and Max Armstrong's mansion spoke eloquently of the difference between Clare's father and the insurance giant of Flagstaff.

Bill Pemberton had always proclaimed that he wouldn't trade his little Victorian bungalow for all the fancy houses in Flagstaff Fairways. Along with his pronouncement he'd subtly implied that wealth could only be gained by unscrupulous means. Yet Max Armstrong seemed more full of scruples than a choir boy. Was he putting up a front for her benefit?

She found her mother in the kitchen baking banana bread to distribute among the neighbors. Edna Pemberton kept her stove busy year-round by baking treats for her family and anyone else in a five-mile radius who acted the least bit friendly. She was slicing bananas rapid fire in time to the rock music from Joel's stereo upstairs.

"If you can hear the music that well down here, what's it doing to his ears up in the bedroom?"

"Clare, what a pleasant surprise!" Her mother stopped gyrating to the music and gave her daughter a hug. She was a good five inches shorter than Clare. Her children had inherited height from their father and fair coloring from her. Edna Pemberton's blond hair disguised the gray, and she looked younger than fifty-one.

"I've given up on the volume of Joel's music," she said, gesturing toward the ceiling. "It seems like the least of my worries with him. He's up there cramming for a chemistry test with a six-pack of Jolt cola, that stuff with double the caffeine in it."

"Great. He can ruin his ears and get the jitters, all at once. Was I like that at seventeen?"

"No, you've always been more sensible. You might have been able to go right into the agency after high school, but Joel just can't. It would be a disaster."

Clare smiled to herself. Joel couldn't create more of a disaster than his mother had in her two-day stint at the agency. "He's going to college, mom. I'm determined he will."

"So am I. Oh! How could I forget? You had your big appointment this afternoon, didn't you? How do things look?"

"I'm not sure, but that's why I'm here. In order to get this account I have to go to Durnberg's other resort in Florida, and I wondered if you—"

"Of course I'll fill in."

"Thanks, Mom."

"I'll enjoy it. I had a good time in your office, meeting all those lovely people. They seemed to appreciate the home-baked goodies I brought in, too. Everyone left with some cookies and a smile."

That's not all they left with, Clare thought. Her mother had discounted everyone's insurance who came through the door, especially if they'd praised her cooking. She told Clare later that she considered it good business to have sales now and then.

"I'd appreciate it if you could watch the office, Mom, but you don't have to do anything with my clients this time. Just answer the telephone and take messages, okay? In fact, why don't you call me if you have any questions? I'll give you the number at the Sugar Sands Resort."

Her mother glanced at her. "Will you be seeing Ron?"

"I don't know. I'll call him tonight and tell him I'll be in town. I suppose it would be a good idea to sit down and go over everything in person." Clare hadn't given Ron much thought since Durnberg announced the trip to Florida, but of course Ron was a factor. Without him she wouldn't have become licensed in Florida so easily and wouldn't have been able to cover both resorts. Ron was an important link in this deal, but Clare had counted on transacting her business by telephone. Meeting former fiancés could be awkward.

"I'd say you owe him at least a dinner or something," her mother suggested, returning to her slicing of the bananas.

"I guess."

"When this all came up, I wondered if you two—"

"No, Mom. Ron's not the right guy for me."

"I've always felt a bit guilty, as if you gave up Ron because you thought that you had to stay here and he was headed for Florida."

"No." Clare put an arm around her mother's shoulders. "If I'd been hopelessly in love with Ron, I would have gone to Florida. Trust me."

"Oh, I do." Her mother frowned. "Clare, you won't have to pay for all this yourself, will you?"

"No, I'll be Durnberg's guest."

"That's a relief, but of course once you get this account we won't have to worry about money so much anymore. And if he's asked you to go there with him, he must be seriously considering your agency."

"Um, he's asked Max Armstrong along, too."

"What? How rude!"

"Just business, Mom," Clare said, hoping it was true. "He wants to compare our programs while he's taking care of whatever problems cropped up in Florida."

"Well, you watch out for that Max Armstrong. He's a wheeler-dealer."

Clare leaned against the counter and gazed at her mother. "Do you know him, Mom? I mean, personally?"

"Never cared to. Anyone who parades his money the way he does, driving Porsches and living in the ritziest section of town, wouldn't be someone I'd want to know personally. He snatched business right from under your father. That's the kind of man he is."

"Mom, I—oh, never mind."

"What, dear?"

Clare realized she'd been about to defend Max Armstrong's character to her mother, to tell her that Max believed in the philosophy of Thumper's father. What had he done to her that she'd become his champion so quickly? Soon she'd sound like Joel. "I was wondering what we have in the way of suitcases," she asked instead.

"Goodness, don't you have one?"

"Mom, I don't take many trips."

"That's true, dear, and I'm delighted you have this chance. Don't worry about a thing at the office. I'll handle everything."

"The best thing to do is take a whole bunch of messages. Don't try to work with the computer. You don't have to handle anything, really. And Mom, no—"

"I know. No sales. All right, but you must admit I brought in all kinds of business for you."

"And I lost most of them when I had to go back and collect more premium."

"I don't understand why the company wouldn't absorb that, Clare. After all, their volume of business increased."

"Mom, just promise me you'll take messages and leave everything for me to do when I get back, okay?"

"Of course, dear. Don't worry about a thing. Just concentrate on outwitting that Max Armstrong. He's a schemer, but I think you can beat him. Much as I hate to admit it, your father wasn't the best businessman in the world."

Clare wondered how her mother could accuse Max of unfair business practices and in the same breath concede that her husband hadn't been good at his job. The blame for Bill Pemberton's failures didn't seem to belong with Max, although that concept was hard for Clare to digest after all the years of conditioning that Max Armstrong was the villain in their lives.

"I'm not going to say if Dad was a good businessman or not, and I can't vouch one way or the other for Max Armstrong's character," Clare said, watching her mother spoon the banana bread batter into three loaf pans. "But I'll do all I can to take Durnberg away from him."

Edna scraped the last of the batter from the bowl into the pans. "But you'll be polite, won't you dear? Please don't forget your breeding."

Clare groaned. How typical of her mother to worry about manners, even when so much was at stake. "Yes, Mom, I'll be polite," she replied.

THE NEXT MORNING, thousands of feet in the air, Clare wondered just how polite she had to be. Durnberg had just offered her a Bloody Mary. Max had already agreed to drink one with his buddy Ham, and Clare had the option of joining them to prove she could handle alcohol at 6:30 a.m. as well as they, or refusing, which possibly would underline her position as an outsider in this gathering. She decided to accept the drink and nurse it for the entire trip.

"So, when did you begin chartering private jets, Ham? Is business that good?" Max asked after the flight attendant brought their drinks. He'd removed the Western sport coat he'd worn to the airport and now looked like a man ready for a vacation in his open-necked, kelly-green knit shirt.

Clare had taken one look at Max when he'd arrived on the runway with a slim garment bag slung over one shoulder and no evidence of a briefcase, and had known that her gray business suit, large suitcase and bulging briefcase appeared pompous in comparison. But she couldn't change the suit and had decided to keep the briefcase, pompous or not, with her during the plane ride. Maybe Durnberg would grab the flight time to glance through her proposal. She hoped that he would.

Still she wished that she'd dressed more casually and brought a smaller suitcase. Max had the advantage, of course, because he'd been to Sugar Sands before and knew what to expect. Besides, he didn't have to go loaded down with facts and figures. He was the incumbent. She needed lots of ammunition to pry him loose from Durnberg, but she didn't want to appear overprepared and stuffy, either. That was another reason, she decided, to pretend enjoyment of the Bloody Mary.

"Business is excellent," Durnberg said, answering Max's question, "but I chartered the jet this morning because this company has been after me to try their service and they offered an introductory deal." He looked pleased with himself. "I thought this would be a good time to take them up on it, so we can all get better acquainted."

Once again Clare picked up the condescension in his tone, as if she and Max were children, and not particularly bright ones, either. The three of them sat in an area where a pair of seats faced each other with a small table in the middle. Clare had chosen a place by the window, and Ham had taken the aisle position diagonally across from her. That had left Max with the option of crawling over Ham to the window seat or settling himself next to Clare. He'd made the obvious choice.

Clare hadn't slept much the night before as images of spending several days in close company with Max jangled her nerves. The reality was worse; she hadn't dealt with such a compelling physical attraction in a while and she struggled to give no sign of it whatsoever to the man sitting next to her. His unruffled behavior made her even more determined to maintain her poise. She would conquer her inappropriate emotions no matter what it took.

Ham nibbled on the celery stick from his drink, which was already half gone. "Tell me, Clare, how is it that such a lovely woman is still single?"

She blinked at the personal nature of the question and immediately thought of all the icy retorts she'd like to make. Instead she sipped her drink and eventually found the resources to smile. "I'm a particular woman, Ham," she said. "My standards are extremely high."

"Ah." Ham winked at Max. "I like women with taste, don't you, Max?"

With her peripheral vision Clare noticed a slight tensing of Max's jaw and wondered how much Max truly cared for his "buddy" Ham Durnberg. The suspicion that he didn't like Durnberg brought her closer in spirit to Max, which didn't help her detachment any.

Despite what Clare imagined was a sign of Max's irritation, he responded to Ham with smiling congeniality. "I sure do like women with taste, Ham. Trouble is, the more taste they have, the less they like me."

Durnberg shook his head. "Max, Max, you're among friends, so you can forget the false modesty." He turned to Clare. "Back in high school this guy was known as 'The Legend,' and the girls he'd dated became known as 'Armstrong's Army.'"

"How impressive," Clare murmured, not quite sure how to respond to Ham's revelations. She didn't doubt that Max had made hearts flutter wherever he went. He'd had that effect on her in short order.

"Perhaps I should mention," Max said, taking a hefty swig of his drink, "that Ham loves the world of make-believe. Whenever he forgot his lines in a play he'd make something up, quick as a wink. He has a tremendous imagination."

"But not this time, Max old buddy. If Adele were here she'd back me up. She tells a great story about all the women who cried like babies at the wedding, when you and Adele got married, and they weren't tears of happiness, either."

"Say, Ham," Max said, leaning forward. "How's your tennis game? Ready to take me on again when we get to Longboat Key?"

Clare admired Max for switching topics. A lesser man might have basked in the praise of his virility, but Max seemed uncomfortable with it.

Durnberg fastened to the new subject with obvious relish. "You're a dead man this time, Max. I've been thinking of registering my backhand as a lethal weapon." Ham glanced at Clare. "You notice how Max weaseled out of our other conversation? That's because he doesn't want you alerted to his reputation with the ladies. He'd rather appeal to your sympathy, is my guess, and tell you how lonely he's been since his divorce. Don't believe a word of it, Clare. The man's dangerous."

"Ham," Max began, a threatening edge to his tone, "I'd rather not discuss—"

"Hey!" Ham threw up both hands and grinned. "Just kidding, old buddy. How about a friendly game of gin rummy to while away the trip?"

Max finished his drink. "Sure, why not? Got any more of these?"

"An endless supply, Max, old boy." Ham signaled the flight attendant and after checking with Clare, ordered two more Bloody Marys and a deck of cards.

Clare could sense Max's effort to relax and shake off the irritation of Durnberg's needling. At one time she'd thought her problem was a long-standing friendship between these two men. Instead, judging from the last exchange, they had a long-standing feud, at least on Durnberg's side. She was there, she understood now, to make matters even more difficult for Max, but Durnberg probably had no intention of switching agents. He enjoyed his power over Max, a man he'd envied in high school and perhaps still did.

Yet Durnberg was a shrewd businessman or he wouldn't have achieved his current level of success, Clare told herself. In the final analysis, wouldn't he take a better program and forget the petty issues of personality? She would bank on that and hope that Durnberg's business sense would win out over his need to manipulate a rival.

Durnberg played gin rummy with ruthless absorption. Lacking his intensity, Max and Clare lost round after round. As Clare watched Durnberg's glee each time he won a game, she realized that his behavior was what she'd expected of Max before she met him. She wished, for simplicity's sake, that the personalities of the two men were reversed. It appeared that she'd have to work to please a man she didn't like and vanquish one that she did.

A breakfast tray was served to each of them and both men moved on to a third Bloody Mary. Clare hoped that neither Ham nor Max intended to drive when they landed in Florida. Ham was slurring his words just a bit, although Max seemed impervious to the alcohol he'd consumed. Clare attributed it to the difference in size of the two men. Although Ham was almost Max's height, he was much thinner.

She'd worked her way through about half of her drink and was developing a headache. She had to laugh to herself when she thought of her mother waving her off the night before with cries of "Have a nice vacation!" The next few days promised to be some of the most taxing of her life, she decided as Ham laid down another winning hand with a flourish.

"You two are no competition," he complained, standing. "Why don't you practice up while I make a pit stop?"

"I don't think practice will help, Ham," Max drawled, leaning back in his chair and stretching his arms over his head. "You've got all the moves today. What do you say we call it quits?"

Ham grinned. "Got you on the ropes, have I?"

"That you do." Max put his arms down and rested his head against the back of his seat. "Unless Clare wants to keep playing?" he asked, turning his head to gaze at her.

"I give up," Clare said, returning his gaze. When he'd raised his arms over his head she'd had the crazy urge to crawl into his lap and nestle within the protection of those comforting arms. She had the feeling that if she could rest her head against his chest and close her eyes for a few minutes, the pounding in her temples would go away.

"You're both a couple of wimps," Ham announced, still smiling. "Maybe after this trip you'll be in better shape. Well, be good while I'm gone." He turned and headed toward the back of the plane.

When he was out of sight Clare groaned and began massaging her temples.

"If you think this is bad, wait until we land," Max said softly. "It gets worse."

She opened her eyes and looked at him. "Why did you agree to come along, then? Obviously you don't enjoy this, either."

"The answer's easy. He expects me to, and his account is worth the trouble. I think. At least I tell myself that before one of these marathon joyrides. Sometimes, like now, I'm not so sure."

"How can you drink three Bloody Marys first thing in the morning?" she asked, rubbing her temples with the tips of her fingers.

He smiled. "Here, let me."

"No, that's okay. I—" Her words of protest died when he reached over and quietly took her hands away to replace them with his. His gentle pressure was heaven and the heavy thud inside her head diminished. "Thank you," she whispered as he worked.

"Don't mention it. Let me give you a tip about the drinking part of this journey. Take the drinks and get in the habit of carrying them around with you. You'll find somewhere to dump them."

Vaguely she remembered that between games Max had also excused himself. "So you haven't had three Bloody Marys?"

"Not even one whole one."

"And I thought you were just good at holding your liquor," she said, keeping her eyes closed as she absorbed the wonder of his massage.

"I am good at holding my liquor. But I don't use that talent when I'm with Ham unless I have to. Once in a while he'll challenge me to a drinking contest, and then I'm stuck."

"Contests. Is that all life is to him?"

"Could be. But I imagine it's worse when I'm around."

"I had no idea," Clare said, wishing that Max could keep rubbing her temples for the rest of the trip. "I thought you had the inside track because you and Ham were great friends."

"That's what he'll tell you."

"Yes, but I know better. I've seen how you stiffen when he starts with his little jibes."

"Perceptive lady," Max said softly. "And that's all for now. He's coming back."

She opened her eyes and gazed at him. "That was wonderful."

"Anytime."

Slowly Clare faced forward in her seat once more and stared unseeing toward the front of the plane as Durnberg arrived with fresh drinks for himself and Max. She smiled as she heard Max thank Ham for the drink because she knew that it would end up being thrown down the bathroom sink eventually. After the magic of Max's easy touch, she felt warm and cared for, relaxed in a way that she hadn't been in quite a long time. She decided that for the moment, she'd allow herself to forget who Max was and what he represented.

4

CLARE STOOD BY THE CURB at the Sarasota-Bradenton Airport and turned her face up to the sun. In spite of her determination to focus on business, she found herself becoming excited about spending a few days on the beach. Perhaps it was because of her prolonged working stretch with no vacation, she thought, but she hungered for this change of scenery in a way she hadn't expected.

A late-model Mercedes with a driver arrived for them, canceling Clare's fears that Durnberg might decide to chauffeur them to the resort himself. Although he seemed amazingly sober, Clare wouldn't have trusted his reaction time behind the wheel for a minute.

Ham took the front passenger seat for himself and ushered Max and Clare into the back seat. She tried to pretend to herself that it didn't matter that she had another chance to be close to Max, but it did. It already did.

He put his arm casually over the back of the seat and brushed her hair. "Sorry," he said, without changing position. "I like to stretch out, if you don't mind."

"No, I don't mind." She realized that she wouldn't mind if he pulled her close and kissed her, either, but of course that was unthinkable. Yet she was thinking it.

She wondered if the trip in a private jet and now a ride through the palm-lined streets of Sarasota in a

Mercedes were altering her perception of reality. If she allowed herself to dream, she'd transform her reason for being here from business to pleasure. How sweet life would be, Clare mused, if she and Max were casual strangers who had happened to meet while vacationing on Longboat Key.

She reached for the automatic window button and glanced at Max. "Do you mind if I open this? I want to smell the salt air."

"Good idea," Max said, lowering his window at the same time.

"Mmm. Wonderful," Clare said, taking a deep breath as the breeze ruffled her hair. "The temperature is perfect." *Everything is perfect*, she thought, *except for our purpose in being here.*

"November's usually very nice," Max said. "Ever been to Florida?"

"No."

Ham hung his arm over the front seat and twisted around in surprise. "Really, Clare? Then we'll have to give her the royal treatment, won't we, Max?"

"You certainly know how to do that, Ham," Max said. "I'll leave the details to you."

No, don't! Clare wanted to cry out, but she didn't. Something told her she'd love the royal treatment if Max planned it, but Durnberg was another story.

"Well, then," Ham said, obviously relishing his control, "I thought we'd start you two out with some tennis while I clear up the little problems that brought me here in the first place. I called to check the schedule before we left Flagstaff and there's a tournament this afternoon. What level of play are you, Clare?"

"I have no idea."

"But you play?"

"Yes, some."

"Better put you in C," Ham said with a wink at Max. "My old buddy will go into A, of course, unless you've deteriorated, Max?"

"As a matter of fact, I have," Max said. "You'd better put me down in C, too. My tennis elbow's acting up again."

Ham frowned. "I thought you challenged me to a match while we were on the plane?"

"The challenge still stands," Max said with a smile.

A flash of anger crossed Ham's aristocratic features before he returned the smile. "Can you believe the ego on this guy?" he said to Clare. "He thinks, even injured, he can beat me."

"Now, Ham, I didn't mean that at all," Max drawled. "I can hold up for one match, but if you put me in a tournament against your top players I'll end up competing in a whole lot of games, and I won't be able to lift a racket, let alone give you a run for your money later."

"Oh. I see what you mean. Okay, C level it is."

Clare was fascinated with the verbal sparring between the two men, and she didn't doubt for a minute that Max had intended to insult Ham. Over the years Max had apparently learned how to deal with Ham's manipulative behavior with some psychological guerilla tactics of his own.

Imagining the next few days in the company of these two, Clare felt as if someone had dropped her into a gladiator pit with no armor to protect her from chance blows from the combatants. No, that wasn't entirely true, she thought. Max would watch out for her. He'd already proved that more than once. She had to deal with the confusing fact that he was her enemy and her friend all wrapped in one.

Ham acted as tour guide, pointing out the gilded magnificence of Ca' d'Zan, former residence of circus magnate John Ringling, and the Sarasota Jungle Gardens. Clare, used to a region where water was scarce, focused primarily on the sparkling water of Sarasota Bay. When they crossed a narrow strip of land leading to Longboat Key, she caught her first glimpse of the Gulf of Mexico and sighed with delight.

Max smiled at her as if to share in her pleasure.

"I'm mesmerized by all this water," she explained, and he nodded. "Maybe I've been landlocked too long."

Max started to reply but Ham jumped into the conversation before he could speak.

"We have a full complement of water sports available at Sugar Sands, Clare," Ham said. "You can have your choice of windsurfing races, deep-sea fishing, snorkeling, parasailing—"

"How about plain old swimming and lying on the beach?" Clare asked. "Or gathering shells and watching sunsets?"

"Well, certainly, but you don't go to a resort for that, now do you? You might as well take advantage of the equipment we have when it's offered free of charge."

"I see what you mean." Clare glanced briefly at Max and caught his amused expression. "Perhaps I should also ask you, Ham, when you'd like to look over my proposal?"

"We'll get to it," Ham said with a dismissing wave of his hand. "Don't worry about that right now. Just have some fun and forget about business, both of you."

Clare gritted her teeth. Ham had adopted his you-two-run-along-now tone. She wondered if he'd ever treat her like a professional, or if this entire trip would be nothing but a game played between Durnberg and Max, with her presence an added twist to their competition. Clare thought of the hours she'd spent on the proposal, of her efforts—with Ron's help—to become licensed in Florida. She would present her program, by God, if she had to do it while she and Durnberg parasailed side-by-side over the sapphire waters of the Gulf.

"Here we are," Ham announced, as the Mercedes entered a narrow, secluded roadway lined with palms and bright flower beds.

The low wooden sign at the entrance to the road demonstrated tasteful understatement, a valued quality on Longboat Key, Clare had decided during the drive. She couldn't imagine how someone like Durnberg managed to fit into the gentle ambiance of this place. In her estimation his style was too brash, too competitive for the area, but then, he'd only owned Sugar Sands for two years. Perhaps his personality hadn't made itself felt yet.

The short entrance road quickly became a circular drive that took them under an elaborate covered entryway. Through breaks in the whitewashed buildings topped with red mission tile, Clare glimpsed the white sand for which the resort was named and the turquoise waters of the Gulf. "Beautiful," she murmured.

"Take time to enjoy it," Max advised from beside her. "Business isn't everything."

She glanced at him and wondered if he'd said that for her benefit or his. Then, already tired of examining motives, she smiled. "I'll try to remember that."

"I'll hop out here and check in with my people," Ham said as the driver coasted to a stop in front of the double entry doors. "Santiago will take you around to your rooms and see that you're both settled." He got out of the car and leaned down to peer in at them. "If I were you I'd order a quick lunch from room service and then run right out to the tennis courts. The tournament starts in an hour."

"I don't have a racket," Clare said, suddenly remembering what the game required and hoping that she'd found a way out of playing.

"No problem," Ham said. "Stop by the pro shop and pick one out. You can charge it to me."

"Oh, Ham, I couldn't possibly—"

"Of course you could." He revealed his perfectly straightened teeth. "You can't play the game if you don't have what you need, right?"

Clare understood his double meaning perfectly. "Right," she agreed. "Thank you for your generosity."

"Don't mention it. Well, see you both later. Santiago, cottage twenty-four is the lady's and twenty-five the gentleman's. Make sure everything's in order, will you?"

"Yes sir, Mr. Durnberg."

Ham turned away from the car and Santiago put it in gear.

"Nice try," Max said as they rode down a winding drive past duplex-styled accommodations. "My racket will be waiting in my room. Ham keeps one here for me so that I'll never have an excuse not to play."

"I've never encountered anyone like this," Clare said in a low voice, hoping Santiago couldn't hear. "And I thought one round of golf on his course would prepare me."

"Don't worry. He doesn't expect you to be very good. I'm the one who's supposed to give him competition."

"I'm not sure that's true. I have this terrible feeling that my success at selling Durnberg might be tied in with my skill at sports while I'm here."

Max gazed at her. "I doubt that. Sports are the obvious thing, but demonstrating skill in any game will impress Durnberg."

"Oh? And what games are you good at, Max? Excluding sports, that is. I've watched you play the drinking game, and the deflecting conversation game. What else is in your repertoire?" To her surprise, Max sighed and glanced away.

"You know, Clare, I'm mighty tired of it all, to tell the truth."

She didn't have a reply to such a weary statement. This might be the chink in Max's armor, she thought. Perhaps what she'd taken for confidence was merely exhaustion, and Max was halfway hoping that she'd take this account from his shoulders. That would explain why he hadn't become licensed in Florida or offered Durnberg the life and health insurance options she'd worked into her program.

Santiago parked the Mercedes behind a whitewashed duplex that carried the number twenty-four over one door and twenty-five over the other. She and Max would be close neighbors, Clare noticed as Santiago helped her out of the car.

"If you'll give me my key, Santiago, I can do this myself," Max said, striding around the car. "You know how much I hate to be fussed over."

"That's fine with me, Max," the swarthy man said, handing Max his garment bag. "Just so you don't tell the boss I didn't carry your suitcases or turn down your covers."

Max laughed. "You know better than that. How's Rosa?"

"Expecting again," Santiago said with a broad grin. "At this rate she'll never get her degree, but she can't decide if she wants to be an engineer or a mother."

"She can be both," Clare said, surprising herself by entering the conversation. She'd been entranced by Max's rapport with the chauffeur and had spoken as if all three of them were old friends.

"I've told her that, too," Santiago said, including Clare naturally in the exchange. "But Rosa doesn't think anyone can raise those kids but her. So what am I going to do?" He shrugged.

"It's a common problem," Clare agreed. "Here, let me take my own suitcases, too."

"Nope." Santiago swung her heavy luggage from the trunk. "This stuff weighs a ton, and I have some standards, you know."

Clare laughed. "I overpacked. I'm sure Max has the right idea."

Santiago glanced at Max and nodded. "Stick around this guy and you'll be okay. Now let's get you settled in your cottage. See you around, Max."

"You bet, San."

As Clare followed Santiago through the door she contrasted Santiago's remark about Max with Durnberg's warning on the plane. Durnberg had told Clare that Max was dangerous, while Santiago had indicated that Max could be her protector. Of the two men giving advice, she instinctively trusted Santiago more. Could she trust his evaluation of Max?

Then Clare forgot about her problems as she looked through the glass front of the cottage to a whitewashed deck and beyond that, nothing but sand, water and sea gulls.

"Shall I put your things in the bedroom, Miss?" Santiago asked.

"That's fine," she said hurrying toward the sliding door that led to the deck. "And please call me Clare," she added over her shoulder as she flipped open the lock and stepped onto the deck. "Wow," she murmured, crossing to the railing and resting both hands on its warm surface. The beach, she could see now, was in two tiers, with a rocked retaining wall holding the top section, where the cottages perched, and wooden steps with railings leading down to the moist sand near the waterline.

Clare leaned down and took off her left shoe. As she was about to remove the right one, Max spoke from just behind her.

"If you're considering a walk on the beach, there's no time."

She turned, holding the first shoe. In a glance she recognized what she hadn't noticed before, that this deck belonged to both unit twenty-four and twenty-five. Although a token railing ran down the middle, Max hadn't had any trouble swinging his long legs over it.

Clare looked down at the low-heeled pump in her hand. "I'd forgotten about the tournament," she said, squinting back up at Max. "Who wants to play tennis when all this—" she swept her arm toward the beach "—is waiting to be explored? Of course, you've been here before, so you probably aren't as excited about beachcombing."

Max smiled. "Who says?"

"I suppose Ham won't be very happy with us if we don't follow his program." Clare felt the same guilty excitement she'd experienced the one time in her life when she'd skipped school to go shopping with some girlfriends.

"No, I don't suppose he will. Want to chance it?"

Clare considered for a moment. If both of them disregarded Durnberg's command to play in the tennis tournament, it would hurt both of their causes equally. Besides that, Clare resented the idea of being Durnberg's puppet, no matter how much this account was worth. Her carefully prepared program was the important thing, not her tennis arm.

"To heck with the tournament," she said. "I'm heading for the beach as soon as I change clothes."

Max's tawny eyes lit with approval. "Meet you back here in five minutes. If you want to put on your suit, we might even decide to swim."

"But no races," Clare added.

"No races," Max agreed and vaulted over to his side of the deck.

Back in her living quarters Clare looked more closely at her surroundings. *Some cottage*, she thought. A plush sofa upholstered in white with teal throw pillows was arranged opposite a fireplace with a driftwood-gray mantel. The rest of the furniture in the room, two easy chairs, a glass-topped dining table and four straight chairs, were all white enameled wicker with patterned pillows in teal, peach and white. There was a small but serviceable kitchen, a gleaming bathroom with gold-plated faucets, and a bedroom. The bedroom furniture was also white, and the spread on the king-size bed matched the pillows on the dining and easy chairs.

Clare wandered about, touching everything with the pleasure of someone unused to luxury. Before changing into her suit she decided to wash her face and hands in the shell-shaped sink. From a wicker basket on the counter she took a bar of gentle soap and unwrapped it while she took inventory of the other supplies. She found the usual lotion, shampoo, sunscreen and shower cap. The Sugar Sands Resort went one step further, however. Clare put down the soap and picked up a small box of condoms.

"Clare? You about ready?"

Clare jumped. Opening a vanity drawer she tossed the box inside and hurried out of the bathroom. Max, his trunks on and a towel over his shoulders, was standing by the open door leading to the deck. Looking at him half-clothed like that, after what she'd just held in her hand, made her face heat and her heart pump. "Come on in," she managed to say. "I'll only be a minute."

She hurried into her bedroom and closed the door without bothering to see if he had followed her suggestion. As she quickly took off her clothes and pulled on her one-piece suit she tried to be rational about the condoms. She'd heard that top-rated hotels were providing such things these days. Just because she had a supply, and no doubt Max also had a supply, didn't mean anyone had to use them.

Yet the idea of making love to Max had been hovering nearby in her subconscious, waiting for the chance to be acknowledged, she realized. He'd attracted her from the beginning and now they were living side by side in an idyllic setting, and some thoughtful soul had provided birth control. She wondered if it was all a coincidence or part of Durnberg's gamesmanship. In either case, circumstances were bringing her dangerously close to an intimate involvement with Max Armstrong.

Clare grabbed her white lace coverup to wear over her red suit. Her hands, she noted, were shaking.

5

THIS WHOLE THING is a setup, Max thought as he stood in the living room waiting for Clare to change into her swimsuit. Dangling his wire-rimmed sunglasses in one hand, he gazed out through the sliding glass door to the sun-kissed waters of the Gulf. *What fun for Ham*, he mused, *watching me try to beat this woman in business and seduce her at the same time.*

Max had been suspicious from the moment Clare had entered Ham's office in Flagstaff. Then had come the Florida invitation for both of them, and now adjoining cottages in this idyllic setting. The condoms in the bathroom might be standard procedure now—it'd been a while since he'd stayed in a resort—but Max had a feeling they'd been placed there deliberately at Ham's request.

Everything taken together spelled out conspiracy. When Max had applied the final test and tried the doors connecting his cottage with Clare's, he'd known for sure what Ham had in mind. Both doors were unlocked.

He'd debated whether to mention the unlocked doors to Clare. She didn't know Ham the way he did, and she might think Max was paranoid to interpret such a small thing as part of a plot to bring them together. The adjoining cottages could be explained as being more convenient for Ham, knowing that Clare and Max were in one spot. As for the condoms, Max didn't think he and Clare were ready to discuss the meaning of that yet.

He could, of course, have thrown the package of Trojans in the wastebasket. He could have locked his door and taken the opportunity while she was in the bedroom to lock hers. By taking action, he could have refused to play along with Ham's manipulations.

Yet he hadn't, partly because she tempted him so, and partly because he thought that he might be able to help her through this. If she needed a shoulder to cry on after Ham dismissed her program as insignificant, he'd like to provide that shoulder.

Max heard the quiet click of a doorknob and turned toward the sound. As he saw her standing there, a long-legged blonde dressed for the beach, sunglasses pushed to the top of her head, body sleek as an otter in her one-piece suit hardly disguised by the lace coverup, Max had the urge to provide Clare with more than a shoulder to cry on. Whether this opportunity had been given to him by E. Hamilton Durnberg or by fate, he'd be a fool to pass it up.

"We have a challenge ahead of us," he said, gazing at her.

She smiled uncertainly. "You mean keeping Durnberg happy while doing what we want?"

"No. We can probably manage that one. I meant something more personal. Something to do with you and me. I'd like us to be friends."

Clare adjusted the strap of her tote bag more securely over her shoulder. "I'd . . . I'd like that too, but we're after the same account Max. Won't that get in the way?"

"Maybe not, if we make a promise that whoever loses the account won't be upset with the winner."

"You're saying that because you expect to win."

He looked into the clear green of her intelligent eyes. "Possibly."

"At least you're honest about it."

"Clare, in my opinion Durnberg brought you down here on a lark. It's a rotten way to treat people and I don't like him much for it, but here we are. Yeah, I think Durnberg will keep his account with me, because he enjoys ordering me around too much to give up that pleasure. But I hope that won't ruin the chance of us being friends."

Clare smiled. "You're so sure of yourself. I wonder if you've considered how you'll feel if the tables are turned and Durnberg takes my program. Will you be *my* friend in that case?"

"Of course I will. I've told you how I feel about business dealings. None of it has to be personal."

"Then I guess nothing will stand in the way of friendship, will it? I'm not a poor loser, and neither are you. It's settled."

Max hoped that she meant what she said. He'd know soon enough, but in the meantime perhaps he could cement his position enough to withstand the strain when she didn't get the account. "Then let's hit the beach," he said, putting on his sunglasses and holding out his hand.

"Sounds good to me." Clare pulled her glasses down over her eyes and nestled her hand in his.

Max was surprised at her unexpected nonchalance toward holding his hand. The friction of her palm sliding over his did funny things to his heartbeat, but he closed his fingers around her hand with a show of unconcern and they started out through the open door.

Before they had reached the stairs leading down to the sand, Clare's telephone rang. They turned together and looked back at the empty living room with its shrilling messenger.

"Damn," Max said. "Could be Durnberg. Want to let it ring?"

Clare released his hand and started back. "I would if I knew for sure it was Durnberg, but I left instructions for my mother to call me if she had any problems at the agency. This could be her."

Max sighed and followed her back through the sliding door. "If it's Durnberg, what will you say?"

"I don't know. I'm a terrible liar."

"Want me to answer?"

She glanced at him. "Why? Are you a good liar?"

"No, but I'm ready to tell Durnberg that we don't want to play in his dumb tournament."

"Dangerous talk, Max. Better let me answer." She picked up the receiver. "Hello?"

"Oh, Clare, thank goodness," her mother said. "I was afraid they were ringing the wrong room, or that I didn't have the resort's number right, or—"

"Mom, what is it?" Clare mentally raced through the possibilities—a bolt of lightning had destroyed the computer; vandals had ransacked the office and dumped paint on all the files; the water pipes had burst and flooded the office . . .

"Your pothos is dying, Clare."

"My *what*?"

"Your pothos. The leaves are yellow and most of them have already fallen off. It's so far gone that I wonder if anything will save it."

"Mother, you called me to say that my office plant is sick?"

"Well, of course, dear. Something has to be done about the poor thing right away, although to tell you the truth I'd advise giving it a decent burial and buying a new one, or perhaps several new plants. Your office needs the oxygen, Clare, not to mention the softening effect of plants. I had no idea that you'd let this one get in such bad shape. What do you want me to do?"

Clare took off her sunglasses and tapped them against her bare thigh as she strove for patience. Knowing how her mother felt about plants, she should have anticipated this and replaced the one in her office which was, she'd admit, suffering for lack of care. What she'd really wanted was artificial plants, but they were much more expensive than live ones. "Mom, if you'd like to buy a few small plants for the office, go ahead. I'll reimburse you when I come home."

"Wonderful, dear. Such a wise decision. Is everything all right there?"

Clare studied Max's broad back as he stood by the sliding door. She followed the line of his backbone, a straight path that led from the white towel draped around his neck to the elastic band of his black swim trunks. She had the urge to run her moist finger over his spine. "Yes, Mom, everything's fine."

"You're keeping an eye on that Max Armstrong, I hope?"

"Yes I am, Mom." Clare smiled.

"Good. Have you called Ron yet?"

Clare's amusement vanished. "No, not yet." Anxiety pricked her sense of well-being as she remembered that she would have to call Ron sometime, perhaps even meet him for a drink or dinner. She shouldn't have involved him in this, but at the time it had seemed safe enough and she'd known no one else in Florida.

"When you do talk to Ron," her mother continued, "give him my best."

"I will. Are there any other problems you needed to talk to me about?"

"Not yet, dear," her mother said cheerfully. "I'll let you go, now. You probably have important meetings this afternoon."

"Well . . . yes."

"Good luck with that Max Armstrong."

Clare wondered what her mother would say if she knew her daughter's plans for the afternoon. "Thanks, Mom. Goodbye."

"Goodbye, dear."

Clare hung up the phone and crossed the living room to where Max stood. "My mother," she explained.

Max turned his head. "Problems?"

"Not really." *Not yet*, she thought and hoped that concern for the houseplants would keep her mother away from the computer and the file cabinet.

"Then let's take off before the damned thing rings again," Max said, cupping her elbow and guiding her out the door. "We won't be that lucky twice."

As they descended the wooden steps to the sand and stopped to remove their thongs, Clare imagined the sound of a telephone and cocked her head to listen. "Is that . . . ?" she began.

"No," Max said, and grinned at her as he took her hand. "You're becoming hopelessly conscientious and it has to stop. Come on."

"But I am hopelessly conscientious," she protested, laughing as they raced across the warm sand.

"It'll get you into trouble around here. Ham loves conscientious people. He tries to drive them crazy with his demands."

Clare pulled them both to a stop and retrieved her hand from his grasp. "Are you trying to talk me out of going after this account? Because it won't work." She looked into the mirror of his sunglasses and wished that she could see his eyes.

"I'm not trying to talk you out of anything." Max hesitated. "But maybe I'd like to soften the blow so that when you don't get the account you won't be so disappointed. Durnberg's not a fun client to have."

"I don't care about fun. I want to build up the agency."

He gazed at her silently. Then he muttered what sounded like an oath.

"Max, if I didn't know better, I'd think that you felt sorry for me. Don't. I know what I'm doing and perhaps in the long run you'll be the one in need of sympathy."

He looked at her for a moment longer before his face relaxed into a smile. "Maybe so. In any case, I think we've spent enough time on E. Hamilton Durnberg."

"I agree." Clare took a deep breath of the salty air and swept her arm toward the Gulf. "Just look at this. Sailboats flitting about on the water, sea gulls gliding through the air, puffy white clouds. Paradise."

Max followed her gaze. "Beats the heck out of a sweaty tennis court. Let's walk." He took her hand again and she didn't resist.

"The colors astound me, Max," she said, still entranced by the Gulf. "I had no idea water could be so many different colors, every shade of blue from teal to navy is out there. I suppose that's from differences in depth."

"Partly. I think Ham told me the blue-green color comes from the limestone underneath."

"Beautiful," Clare murmured. "And calm as a bathtub," she added, watching the water ruffle at the edges like the lace on a country girl's skirt. "Is it usually so calm?"

"Let's put it this way. Frankie Avalon and Annette Funicello would have a tough time making a surfing movie on this beach."

"That's fine with me," Clare said, laughing. "I don't know how to surf, anyway. I'll bet you do, though." She glanced at him and was surprised to see his frown. What had she said? But before she could ask he grinned at her as if nothing in the world could upset him.

"What makes you think I'm a surfer?" he teased. "I don't even hum Beach Boys tunes."

Clare started to praise his athletic build and decided against it. "You're an athlete," she said, feeling safe with that statement. "It stands to reason you've tried surfing like any other red-blooded American male who lives within a day's drive of the ocean."

"A few times," he admitted. "But the big sport around here is shelling."

"As in hunting for sea shells? Please don't tell me Ham's made that into a competition, too."

"At dinner he gives a prize for the most unusual find of the day."

Clare groaned. "I can't stand it. Max, is it possible to wander along Ham's beach for no special reason?"

He smiled at her. "I don't know. Pretty daring. Want to try?"

"Yes, please."

"Then follow me. We'll try to set a precedent."

They walked down a narrow wooden stairway that led to the damp sand near the water line. A rock retaining wall about six feet high separated the two levels of beach and gave the lower portion a measure of seclusion.

Although a few sunbathers had been stretched out on the top level, Clare noticed that the bottom section was deserted, possibly because it was lunchtime. At the base of the steps Max suggested that they leave his towel and her totebag inside the steps and explore the beach unencumbered. She agreed.

Clare was used to the vigorous surf and khaki-colored sand of California beaches. After her first few steps across the cool, gray-white sand of the gulf, she stopped. "It squeaks! You'd think I was walking across a warped floor or something."

Max laughed. "That's sugar sand. It makes noise."

"What fun," Clare said, pressing her feet into the resilient surface as she marched along beside Max. "I thought sand was sand, but apparently not. Anyway, I recognize those," she said, pointing to dove-sized birds that skittered around on long, skinny legs as if playing tag with the advancing curls of water. "Those are sandpipers."

"That's right. I suppose you're too young to remember that movie with Elizabeth Taylor and Richard Burton."

"*The Sandpiper*? I saw it on T.V. That's how I learned what kind of bird that is." Clare also remembered the stirring fireside love scene in the film and wondered if Max remembered it, too.

"What did you think of that movie?" he asked.

Clare hesitated. The film was wildly romantic and her answer would reveal a lot about herself. "I...I loved it," she confessed, and glanced away. First *Bambi* and now this. He probably thought she was a sentimental slob.

"So did I," he said quietly.

Her gaze met his but his sunglasses blocked her way. *Just as well*, she thought, and her glance skittered past him, mimicking the erratic paths of the sandpipers. She felt short of breath and dizzy with uncertainty. Was she reading more into his behavior than was there?

She cleared her throat and swerved the conversation back to neutral ground. "What are those holes in the sand?"

"Breathing holes for little sand crabs. They bury themselves under there."

"Really?" Clare knelt on the damp sand and peered at the toothpick-sized holes.

Max crouched beside her. "Want to dig one up?"

"Absolutely not! That little crab deserves his privacy." She noticed Max's smile. Was he patronizing her? "I suppose you think I'm pretty funny, being concerned for the privacy of crabs?"

"I think," he said, helping her to her feet, "that you're pretty wonderful."

Her heart began to pound as she gazed up at him. "Do you?" she asked softly. "It's hard to tell what you're thinking behind those sunglasses."

He reached up and took them off. "Better?"

She nodded. Oh, yes, it was much better, and much more frightening to see the sparkle of admiration and desire in the brown and gold depths of his eyes.

"It isn't fair for you to have the advantage," he said, gently removing her sunglasses and holding them in the same hand with his.

She trembled as if he'd undressed her. She wondered if her emotions flickered in her eyes with the same intensity as his. After a breathless minute he reached for her, and she didn't have to wonder anymore.

Despite the uncertainty of only a few moments ago, moving into his arms was the easiest thing she'd ever done. Resisting would have been the unnatural act. She marveled at how her arms slipped easily over his shoulders as the space between them narrowed.

She tingled in anticipation of the moment when her breasts would encounter the firm wall of his chest. When the moment came, she sighed with pleasure. He drew her closer and the warmth of his groin pressed against her flat belly.

She gazed unflinchingly into his eyes. "I'm not afraid of you," she murmured, and wasn't sure if she'd said it for his benefit or hers.

"I don't want you to be."

"This doesn't change anything." She caught the flash of amusement in his expression. "About the account," she added.

"I don't expect it to."

"Just so you don't think that—"

"I don't think anything," he said, lowering his head. "Especially when I'm doing this."

There was no question about the kiss. Clare hungered for it, even as she'd tried to establish ground rules before it happened. As his lips found hers, the whisper of the waves seemed to grow louder in her ears.

His mouth was supple and more sensuous than she would have imagined possible. His kiss moved beyond gentle exploration to become a promise of how he would love her if given the chance. Clare abandoned her usual caution and surrendered to the persuasion of his lips, the insistence of his tongue. He would read compliance in her kiss; he would expect more after a response like this, but she couldn't help herself. He tasted of a passion that she longed to know.

She lost track of where she was until a ripple of water swirled over her feet. Startled, she drew back. "The water," she said in a strangled voice.

"It doesn't matter." He smiled. "The water's warm."

She realized that he was right. The gentle waves caressing her feet had no bite at all. Like his kisses, they promised only pleasure. As the waves withdrew, they pulled sand from under her feet like a loose rug, and she clutched Max for support.

"I'm here," he said, holding her tight.

"I know." With a sigh she closed her eyes as his breath mingled with hers once more. Just before the exquisite pressure of his lips settled against her mouth she heard the high-pitched giggle of a child. They were no longer alone.

Max released her and together they turned toward the sound, which had come from the bottom of the steps where a blond girl of about four stood watching them. She was hanging onto the railing, poised there as if following instructions to go no farther. Her umbrella and towel-laden mother appeared at the top of the stairs and began making her way down one step at a time after glancing with curiosity at Max and Clare.

"Let's swim," Max said in a low tone.

"Yes, let's." Clare untied her lace coverup and tossed it to the dry sand beyond the water line. Then she took the hand Max offered and ran with him into the welcome haven of the water.

"Take a deep breath," Max instructed when they were waist-deep. "We're going under."

Without stopping to think Clare dove beneath the turquoise water and found herself once more in his arms and tasting the excitement of his salt-flavored lips. His body, slick and muscular, entwined with hers and she longed for a mermaid's ability to stay submerged forever. Her breasts, throbbing for his touch, strained against the material of her suit. She pressed against him, willing the barriers to be gone, but the need for air drove them to the surface, still holding each other.

Moisture beaded on his eyelashes as he gazed at her. "I lied," he murmured, pushing her wet hair away from her cheek.

She slid both arms around his waist and leaned back to study him. "About what?"

"You asked if we could walk along Ham's beach for no reason at all, and I said we could. But I had a reason. I wanted you all to myself."

Her voice had a husky ring. "I forgive you for that." She licked the salt water from her lips and saw desire flare in his golden eyes as he watched the motion of her tongue.

Silently he urged her into deeper water, until her shoulders were almost covered. "There's more I need to be forgiven for," he said softly, rubbing his fingers along the straps of her suit. "Having you to myself isn't the end of what I want."

Her heart was thudding but she met his gaze. He fascinated her with his swift, sure pursuit, and his obvious passion sparked needs that she had long suppressed. When his hands moved gently over her collarbone and under the surface of the water she didn't protest. Soon her breasts swelled against the material of her suit and strained to fill his cupped hands. She closed her eyes and tilted her head back with a shiver of forbidden ecstasy as he stroked his thumbs across her nipples imprisoned beneath the wet nylon.

"God, Clare." His hands trembled as he caressed her. "I'm fighting to keep from ripping this thing off you."

He slid both hands back to her shoulders and took a shaky breath. "Wow."

Her eyes fluttered open. "The terrible thing is," she whispered, "that I wouldn't mind if you did."

He groaned. "That's not terrible." He glanced at the beach, which was rapidly filling with swimmers and sunbathers. "But not here. The place is suddenly alive with tourists."

"Max, this is crazy. We're crazy."

"No, we're both sane," he said, leading her out of the water. "Durnberg is the crazy one, treating us like puppets, hoping our attraction to each other will mess with our heads. My head, to be exact."

"Durnberg? You think this is what he wants, for us to become involved?"

Max didn't answer.

"Well, is it?"

They'd reached dry sand and he leaned down to get her lace coverup. "Maybe I'm wrong."

"But what if you're not? Max, I don't like the idea of reacting exactly the way Durnberg wants us to, as if we were part of his high school biology experiment."

He glanced at her. "How about what just happened between us?"

"I'd rather believe it was our idea and not Durnberg's."

"Clare, it *was* our idea. And Durnberg never has to suspect anything."

"You mean, pretend that we're indifferent to each other?"

"That's not a bad idea. It won't be much fun, because I suspect Durnberg plans to be with us most of our waking hours for the next couple of days. I suspect we'll find a message from him when we get back to the cottages. But we can work around him."

"We can? How?"

Max smiled and touched her cheek. "The guy has to sleep sometime."

She gazed up at him, breathless with his implication. "Don't you?"

His golden eyes gleamed with sensuous good humor. "Why, because I'm approaching middle age and need my rest?"

She blushed. "No, but—"

"You know, Clare," he said, rubbing his knuckle along her lower lip, "I think it's time you learned what a forty-two-year-old man can do."

6

CLARE AND MAX WALKED casually back to their rooms as if the passionate kisses hadn't happened. They agreed that their personal interactions were nobody's business but their own, and whether or not Durnberg had plotted to bring them together wasn't really the point.

"I'll walk you to your door and see if your message light is blinking," Max said. "When Ham discovers we're not on the tennis court, I predict that his control-happy mind will start devising ways to bring us back in line."

"From what you've said, I'm amazed that he's left us alone this long."

"Only because he had important business to take care of. Once that's settled, look out. Your life will not be your own."

"I see." As they climbed the steps to her deck, Clare glanced at Max, who was wearing his sunglasses again and looked grim. "And what if the message light isn't blinking?"

He paused with a hand on the railing and turned toward her as a slow smile eased the tension from his face. "Well, now, Miss Clare, that's a mighty nice prospect. It means that Ham hasn't caught up with us yet."

Heat spread through her as she realized what he meant. The forbidding expression created by the sunglasses had been transformed by that smile to a rakish appeal that quickened her heartbeat. "I . . . guess we'd better find out which it is," she said, and hurried up the steps ahead of him.

"Nice," he murmured from behind her.

"Pardon?" She took off her sunglasses and searched for the key in her tote bag.

"The way you move. I like watching you."

"Oh." Somehow she found the key, although her hands were shaking and she had trouble unlocking the sliding door. So much would be decided by a simple light on her telephone. If it was blinking, it would signal a probable end to their privacy. If not, she expected Max to lock the door, close the drapes and stay.

As they walked into the room the only sound was Max's muttered oath. The small red light on the telephone was pulsing methodically.

"I'll check mine, too," he said, jerking off his sunglasses in irritation.

Clare swallowed. "We could . . . ignore it."

He crossed the room and took her in his arms. "Thank you for saying that." He gazed with longing into her eyes. "But it won't work. If he's already leaving messages for us he'll get impatient if they're not returned and come pounding on the door." He traced the line of her lips with one finger. "That would be a lousy beginning."

Clare throbbed in response to the pressure of his nearly naked body against her damp swimsuit. She was dazzled by the strength of her physical attraction to him and she wanted reassurance that he experienced the same reckless abandon. "Maybe it's not Durnberg," she said, molding her body to his. "Maybe my mother called again."

"Clare." He spoke her name as a warning and tightened his arms around her.

"Oh, Max, I am afraid of you," she confessed. "I'm afraid of this power you have to make me forget everything else but my overwhelming need for you. I'm scared to death of that, of what could happen if—"

"It's okay," he said, soothing her. "I won't take advantage and sabotage your business dealings with Ham. You may not get the account, but it won't be because of me." He released her and stepped back. "Check your messages and we'll take it from there. In the meantime I'll check mine."

"All right." She watched him walk toward the door connecting the cottages. "Isn't that locked?"

He turned back to gaze at her. "No. Both doors have been open ever since we got here."

"Do you think Durnberg left them that way on purpose?"

"Maybe." He paused. "Want to lock this after me?"

"No."

He smiled and was gone.

Adopting a fatalistic attitude, Clare reached for the telephone and dialed the front desk. She couldn't imagine a message that she would welcome at this moment. Instead, she harbored unrealistic fantasies of spending unlimited time with Max. The man was exciting and the setting was perfect. All she had to do was forget her reason for being here and she could have the time of her life.

"Front desk," answered a pleasant male voice.

"I'd like my messages, please."

"Let's see. For cottage twenty-four I have three. One from Mrs. Pemberton letting you know she's bought seven plants, one from Mr. Durnberg advising you of a reservation he's made in the dining room for six-thirty, and a third from a Mr. Ron Trilling asking you to call immediately."

Clare squeezed her eyes shut. Ron. She'd have to deal with him, probably that afternoon. "Thank you," she told the desk clerk and hung up the phone.

Max rapped on the door frame and stepped into the room. "Well? Did you get the dinner summons? It's better than I thought. Apparently he doesn't expect to see us until six-thirty, and it's only a little past three now."

"Max, I had one more message."

"Your mother?"

"Yes, but also one from a . . . business associate here in Sarasota. I'll have to call him back."

Max's open, eager expression vanished and his look became guarded. "Will you have to see him?"

"I don't know. Maybe."

"Then I suggest you do it this afternoon, before Durnberg latches on to you again."

"Max, I'm sorry. I didn't anticipate—"

"Never mind, Clare. I said that I wouldn't interfere in your business life, and I won't." He gave her a level look. "This is your business life, I take it?"

"Yes."

"Good, because I have a thing about interfering with established relationships. If you're emotionally involved with someone, I'd like to know it now."

His straightforward attitude about other men in her life didn't surprise her; it fit with what she knew of him. "There's no one," Clare said, but felt a little dishonest about Ron and decided to elaborate. "I used to be engaged to this man, but that's been over for a long time. He's in insurance, too. What we have to discuss is purely business."

Max leaned against the door frame. "Something about a license in Florida?"

This man is nobody's fool, she thought. "Yes. Ron helped put that through for me."

"It seems I may have underestimated you after all." Max's smile took the sting out of his words.

"Why haven't you done the same thing, Max?" she asked. Irrational though it was, she was irritated with him for not protecting himself better.

"Flagstaff Fairways was enough for me," he said simply.

"But wouldn't your client be better served to have the same agent for both resorts?"

Max shrugged. "I didn't have a contact in Florida and it would've had to be someone really trustworthy. You obviously have such a contact. That's good. Maybe Ham will split the business and give you Sugar Sands and me Flagstaff Fairways."

"Max, I'm going after both."

Max smiled and shook his head. "You still don't understand E. Hamilton Durnberg. Giving you both of the accounts wouldn't be any fun for him."

"I can't believe that matters so much."

"Believe it." Max pushed himself away from the door. "Well, I'd better let you go. You have things to do and people to see."

"What will you do?"

"Oh, I'll probably wander over to the tennis courts and practice my backhand."

"So you can beat Durnberg?"

"No. To assure myself that I could if I wanted to. See you at dinner." He walked back into his side of their duplex and left both connecting doors open behind him.

Clare went to her bedroom to get Ron's business card with his telephone number on it. Noticing the telephone on the bedside table, she decided to use it. No matter how much she trusted Max, and she trusted him quite a bit, he was still her competitor and didn't need to know every aspect of her proposal for Durnberg.

It was enough that he'd figured out that she was licensed in Florida. Clare felt safe with that disclosure, because Max wouldn't have time to get his own Florida license before she presented her program to Durnberg. Anyway, Max sounded as if such a move didn't interest him. Clare thought he was foolish, but he seemed to believe that Durnberg wouldn't dump him no matter what she presented as an alternative.

Ron's secretary answered the phone and put Clare right through as if she had special instructions to do so.

"Clare? It's good to hear from you!" Ron's voice boomed across the line. "When did you get in?"

"Not too long ago," Clare evaded. "I've been out on the beach."

"Gorgeous, isn't it?"

"Yes." *Especially in the company of the right person,* Clare thought.

"Listen, as long as your friend Durnberg has given us this golden opportunity, let's have dinner while you're here and go over this proposal in person. I have several questions."

Clare wished she'd never begun this collaboration, but it still might prove to be the deciding factor in getting Durnberg's business. "I doubt if I can make it for dinner, Ron. I'm finding out that E. Hamilton Durnberg likes to plan his guests' time carefully and I think I'll be expected to have dinner with him every night."

"He's not trying to put the move on you, is he?"

"No, nothing like that." Clare heard a door close and felt a tug of sadness. Max had left for the tennis courts. "Durnberg's very manipulative," she continued, trying to forget about her lost opportunity to spend time with Max. "This afternoon he had business to take care of, so I have an hour or two free, if you'd like to meet now. Frankly, I think that might be our only chance." She prayed that he already had appointments lined up. She still might be able to catch up with Max.

"Right now?" Ron hesitated. "Sure, I can do that. Give me a few minutes to take care of some stuff and I'll pick you up. What cottage did he give you?"

Clare shook off her disappointment. "I'm in twenty-four."

"Where'd he put your competition?"

"Twenty-five."

"Uh-*huh*. What do you think, Clare? Can you beat the old guy?"

Clare stopped herself from laughing at Ron's "old guy" description. "He's only about forty-two, Ron."

"Is that all? I thought he'd been around forever."

"It seems that way because he got into the business right out of high school."

"No college training? Then you're a cinch to win this one, with all the business courses you've taken."

"I think I can do it, but it won't be a cinch. He's pretty entrenched. Apparently he and Durnberg were in high school together."

"Don't worry about that. Your program looks great. Shall I see you in about twenty minutes, then? We'll get a drink at St. Armand's Circle. Did you pass it on your way to Sugar Sands?"

"Yes, and it looked like a lovely shopping area." Clare tried to pump enthusiasm into her comments when all she wanted was to be with Max. "Sounds terrific, Ron." She consoled herself with the knowledge that this would be the only break in her time with Max. Tonight she'd see him for dinner, and then . . .

"Clare? Are you still there?"

"Yes! Sorry, did I miss something?"

"I was saying that it will be nice to have a drink together again. Like old times."

"Yes, yes it will. See you soon. Bye." She hung up before Ron could blither on about old times anymore. She'd make it through the next couple of hours somehow. Who would have thought that she'd end up having to meet Ron in person again in the same period of time that she was becoming involved with another man?

And she was becoming involved, she admitted as she dashed through a shower and used a blow dryer on her hair. With her free hand she opened the drawer where she'd tossed the condoms. She stared at them for a while and shut the drawer. Then she switched off the dryer.

Wearing only her bra, half slip and nylons, she padded through the open connecting doors and headed for Max's bathroom. There, lying on the counter as if he'd picked them up and tossed them down again, was a box identical to the one in her bathroom cabinet drawer. *Well*, she thought, *if matters become intimate, at least we won't have to go shopping first.*

She'd started back to her side of their living quarters when the outside door opened and Max walked in, carrying a tennis racket and a can of balls. They stared at each other for several seconds until Max recovered enough to close the door and put down the racket and balls.

"Did you need to borrow my safety razor?" he asked, his gaze traveling over the revealing lace of her bra.

"I . . . uh . . . thought you were going to practice your backhand?"

"I decided to come back on the off chance that your business appointment hadn't worked out."

"It did work out. Ron is picking me up in ten minutes." She realized some explanation was called for but she couldn't come up with a plausible fib and the truth stuck in her throat. What would she say, that she was counting condoms?

"Hey, it's no big deal," Max said, walking toward her. "I haven't got any secrets over here, but I'm damned curious why I found you standing in the doorway of my bathroom."

Clare reddened. There was no way out. "I . . . I wondered if the resort had provided you with the same sort of . . . amenities they gave me."

Relief and laughter sparkled in his eyes. "And did they?"

"It seems so." She cleared her throat. "I'd better finish getting ready," she said, starting past him.

"Give me thirty seconds," he said, catching her arm.

"Thirty seconds?"

"Yeah. You can time me. I want to hold you when you're like this, all silk and lace. Proper and improper at the same moment." He drew her into his arms. "Did you know that when you blush, you blush all over? At least, all the parts I could see."

"Max, I didn't imagine that you'd come back. I was only—"

"I'm glad I did." He rubbed a palm over the smooth slip covering her bottom. "Besides, you answered my question. I wondered the same thing."

"Do you think that's standard? Or did Durn-berg..."

"I don't care," Max said, running a finger down the scalloped edge of her bra. "If you like, I'll replace them before we leave."

Her heart raced. "You're that sure that we will—"

He gazed down at her. "Yes, I'm that sure."

"I have to go," she whispered.

"I know. Thank you for my thirty seconds."

She moved away from him, her gaze maintaining the connection, her hand groping for the doorway.

"Go on," he said softly. "Do this. We'll have time, later. We can both pretend that we're exhausted from jet lag and have to turn in early."

In a daze she turned and walked back to her bedroom. Habit guided her movements as she finished putting on her clothes. *Turn in early. Are you sure? Yes.* She reached for the pale green cocktail dress because she thought Max might like it, the gold-looped earrings because they might intrigue him. When Ron tapped on her door, she'd almost forgotten that he was the man picking her up.

"Hey, Clare, you look great!" Ron hugged her before she could stop him. He smelled of the same co-logne she remembered. His blond hair was styled differently, a little longer, but otherwise Ron hadn't changed much in two years.

"Thanks for the compliment." She disentangled her-self as quickly as possible and wondered if Max was still in the other cottage, listening. As far as she knew, the connecting doors were still wide open. Would Ron no-tice and comment? She couldn't look back over her shoulder and check without seeming obvious.

"Nice spot," Ron said, glancing around. "We could always stay here and order room service, if you—"

"No," Clare said quickly. "Let's go out. I haven't seen much of the area, after all."

"Sure." Ron smiled. "Ready to go?"

"Let's see. Have I forgotten anything?" Clare glanced around the room and noticed that her connecting door was closed. Max must have done that for her, knowing that leaving it open for Ron to see would have put her in a compromising position.

"Perhaps your briefcase?" Ron prompted. "Unless you'd rather not talk business. Maybe we should just kick back and forget this proposal. We can always work out another time when you can sneak away, don't you think?"

"No, I don't." Clare hurried into the bedroom and returned with her briefcase. "I expect to be tied up after this afternoon."

"Too bad," Ron said, allowing his disappointment to show. "I'd forgotten what a gorgeous lady you are, Clare. I've been thinking that perhaps I made a mistake, leaving you back there in Flagstaff."

"Ron, we made that decision together, remember? And promised never to reopen the subject and to stay friends."

Ron laughed, a short, harsh sound. "What a lot of horse manure that idea is. I'll tell you two things that don't mix, Clare—business and pleasure, and friendship and sex."

"Then we're not friends?"

Ron opened the door and ushered her out. "What we are, Clare, is business associates."

Clare accepted his statement gratefully and worked for the next two hours to keep their relationship cool and casual. She knew Ron well enough to trust that he wouldn't give up the portion of the Sugar Sands commission that she'd offered him just because she'd rebuffed his romantic advances.

As they talked, she couldn't help thinking about what he'd said, that business and pleasure didn't mix, and neither did friendship and sex. She wondered if the statement was true, and if so, what it meant in relation to her and Max.

What she wanted was a sharp division between her business life, in which she was in competition with Max, and her personal life, in which she was in league with him in search of pleasure. Could it work? And with all that, could they also be friends? Clare admitted to herself that she wanted everything—the account and Max. He'd said the account didn't matter, but then he expected to keep it.

Sometime before six Clare suggested that she and Ron had covered every questionable aspect of the Sugar Sands proposal and she'd appreciate a lift back to her cottage.

"We missed the sunset over the water," Ron said as he helped her out of the car in front of her door. "I'd meant to show you that."

"That's all right." Clare was glad he hadn't. Sharing her first sunset over the Gulf with Ron would have been all wrong.

"You're a hell of a businesswoman, Clare." Ron leaned against the fender of his black Audi. He'd spent part of their time together explaining his complicated lease arrangement, of which he was very proud. "Why not move to Florida and come into the business with me? You've got the license and what difference would it make whether you ran Sugar Sands or Flagstaff Fairways from a distance?"

"The answer's still the same as it was two years ago," she said, noticing for the first time that Ron's eyes were set too close together and he was developing a double chin. She wondered why she had ever found him attractive. "I'm staying to run my dad's agency and help my mother, at least until Joel's out of school."

"There's a wealth of opportunity here, Clare. And you have to admit the place is beautiful."

"So is Flagstaff. And I have ties there."

Ron looked at her speculatively. "Something about the way you said that makes me think a man is involved in your decision. Gonna tell Uncle Ron about it?"

"No. I mean, there's nothing to tell."

"I don't believe you. There's a telltale flush in your cheeks, and I've accepted the fact that I'm not the reason. You're sure Durnberg's not sweet-talking you? Not that it would be such a bad thing, mind you."

"No, he's not. I'm unattached, Ron."

"But tied to Flagstaff."

"By my family," she insisted.

"Right." He looked unconvinced, but he dropped the subject and shrugged. "Well, knock 'em dead when you present this plan. Durnberg would have to be an idiot not to switch his coverage to you."

"Thanks, Ron, for everything. I couldn't have done it without you."

"So you said when you paid for our drinks, but gratitude's a poor substitute for good chemistry. I'm sorry we lost it, Clare."

His honesty brought a twinge of sympathy and the urge to be just as honest. "I really don't think we ever had it," she said gently, thinking of her afternoon with Max.

"Aha! Someone is on the horizon."

"I'm not sure. Maybe." She held out her hand. "Goodbye, Ron. I'll be in touch."

His handshake was brief and crisp. "Great."

She watched him drive away with relief. The rest of her free time in Florida belonged to Max. She turned the key in the lock and wondered if he was in his side of the duplex now, perhaps showering for dinner. The thought gave her goose bumps. She wondered if she could be daring enough to wander into his room, this time knowing he was there, knowing that he could be dressing.

She walked in and immediately noticed that the connecting doors were open again. A lamp was on in her living room, although she hadn't left one burning, and another light glowed from Max's side, but Clare knew from the silence that he wasn't there, after all.

With a sigh of disappointment she wandered into her bedroom, where the lamp was also on. The resort staff could have turned on the lights, Clare thought, but she preferred the idea that Max had done it to welcome her home. A sheet of resort stationery rested on her pillow and she picked it up.

"Dear Clare, I'm in the bar having a drink with Ham. Come on over when you get back—Max"

Clare's first thought, and she didn't like herself much for thinking it, was that Max was getting in a few licks for his program while she wasn't around. Yet she couldn't blame him if that was exactly what he was doing. Perhaps she'd shaken him up a little with the information that she was licensed in Florida and planned to go after both resorts.

She, too, would have to arrange some time alone with Ham. Tonight after dinner might be her first opportunity to present her program. She should suggest it, she thought, and disregard the temptation to hurry back to the seclusion of this room with Max.

After all, Max was protecting his interests and she should protect hers. Right now he was having a drink with Ham in the bar, not sitting here like some puppy dog waiting for her to come home. He had a strategy to keep this account; she must plan one to take it away.

Clare felt strange, plotting against a man who had recently held her tenderly in his arms, but Max himself had issued the challenge of keeping their personal and business interests separate. What had he said when they'd first met? Something about having to mow down a few princes in order to survive, but there was nothing personal in it, he'd said.

Well, Clare thought, she might have to mow down this particular prince, but if he'd been straight with her, the business loss wouldn't affect their relationship. She had no choice except to take him at his word and hope for the best.

After refreshing her makeup and throwing a lightweight coat over her shoulders, she picked up her briefcase and left the cottage. She could check the briefcase at the front desk, she'd decided, and retrieve it if Ham agreed to a meeting after dinner.

Fog blurred the outlines of trees and buildings as she walked toward the clubhouse, guided by knee-high lamps that reminded her of tiny Japanese pagodas. The air was fragrant with salt water and the dank scent of tropical growth along the path.

Not far away the Gulf whispered, and occasionally, through breaks between cottages, she glimpsed fog-

fuzzed lights on the sailboats and cabin cruisers bob-
bing at anchor on the calm water. She envied the people on the boats and imagined them in pairs, lovers
escaping from land to cocoon themselves in cozy privacy.

She pictured herself on such a boat with Max, although the idea was silly. Max had lived most of his life
in Arizona, and he'd have no reason to be knowledge-
able about boats. She was unrealistically connecting
him to this place as if he and not Durnberg had brought
her to Sugar Sands. She considered, although unwill-
ingly, that her sudden and overwhelming attraction to
Max might be fostered by this setting, which was more
sensuous than any place she'd ever known.

For the first time she felt a twinge of embarrassment
for the way she'd so easily abandoned herself to Max.
How much of her response, she wondered, had been the
excitement of a glamorous vacation spot that looked
even more wonderful to someone who had been
chained to her desk for two years? Perhaps her thinking this afternoon had been as blurred as the fog-draped
scenery was tonight.

She entered the bright lobby and checked both her
briefcase and coat at the registration desk before asking directions to the lounge. It was almost six-thirty, but
with luck she'd catch Ham and Max before they left for
the restaurant. Clare wanted her choice of seats at the
table, if possible.

Fishing nets and translucent shells decorated the
lounge, and Clare noticed a number of customers with
colorful tropical drinks in front of them. She spotted
Ham and Max at a far corner table and both were
holding squat glasses of amber liquid and ice. No par-
asols and fruit slices at that table, thought Clare with

a grim smile. She wondered if Max had found some potted plant to dump his drinks in or if this was a case when he'd had to match Ham shot for shot.

From the way they leaned back in their chairs, ties loosened and each with an ankle over one knee, she suspected that at least one of them had consumed a fair share already. She hoped that Ham wouldn't get too looped to understand her program if she presented it after dinner.

She paused for a moment in the shadows to study Max unobserved. Despite her lectures to herself on the way over, the sight of him set off intense yearnings that seemed potent enough to be more than a whim of the time and place.

Although she was enchanted by his slightly irregular smile and his wide-set, laughing eyes, she was emotionally stirred by the strength in his face, his strong nose and jutting chin. His features taken together were rugged and compelling, but she was most attracted by his self-possession, a quality that had struck her first when she'd met him in her office, and radiated from him even here in this dimly lit bar.

If she chose, she could have him all to herself after dinner. They'd already worked out the signal, and watching him now, she ached for the chance to nestle into his arms. She juggled the possibilities in her mind and as she considered them, Max took a pen from an inside pocket of his Western jacket. Grabbing a napkin, he began scribbling something and pushed it across the table toward Ham.

Ham studied what was on the napkin while Clare held her breath. When Ham nodded, she made her decision. After dinner she would tend to business. Max had given her no choice.

7

CLARE THREADED HER WAY through the tables, when Max looked up. The delight in his expression nearly destroyed her resolve to concentrate on business, but she forced herself to think of the writing on the napkin and Max's purpose in being alone here with Ham. Both men rose as she approached, and Ham tucked the napkin in his jacket pocket.

"Just in time," Ham said, pushing back his sleeve to consult what looked to Clare like a Rolex. "And aren't you lovely tonight, Clare."

"Thank you." She glanced at Max and allowed herself the luxury of accepting his unspoken praise. She realized that if Durnberg had been facing Max instead of her, he would have taken one look at Max and guessed that he and Clare were already more than casual friends.

"I think we may as well head for the dining room." Durnberg put a hand at her waist and steered her back in the direction from which she'd come. She clenched her teeth and tried not to flinch at the pressure of his palm against the small of her back. She couldn't believe that in such a short time she'd developed an aversion to the touch of every man except Max, but it seemed to be true.

"Max tells me you've been busy this afternoon, both of you, and ignored my plans for the tennis tournament," Ham said as they negotiated their way through the tables to the lounge entrance.

Clare was glad Max was behind them. If she'd had to look into his eyes she would have blushed. "I had an unexpected call from a business associate of mine who lives in Sarasota," she said over her shoulder.

"So I understand. Did you settle your business with him, then?"

"Yes, thank you."

"Good, because I have a full day planned for the three of us tomorrow. I, too, settled my business this afternoon, so tomorrow we can all relax and play games."

They left the lounge and walked down a carpeted hallway toward the restaurant. Clare imagined that she could calculate within a fraction of an inch the distance between Max's arm and hers as they walked side by side, careful not to touch. She turned her head slightly to enjoy the scent of his after-shave and the faint aroma of bourbon on his breath. The urge to kiss him moistened the inside of her mouth.

Ham stopped briefly to speak with the maître d', and Max took the opportunity to lean in her direction. "You look sensational," he murmured. "Although I like the way you were dressed earlier this afternoon much better."

She had no time to answer him. Ham rejoined them and the maître d' ushered them to a table. She struggled to bring her thoughts under control. The presence of Max only inches away was difficult enough, but he'd had to remind her of that incident when he'd caught her in his bathroom.

Ahead of them, the maître d' indicated a table with one side pushed against the glass wall that faced the water. Spotlights mounted on the roof of the resort illuminated the shoreline and bleached the incoming breakers a startling white. The maître d' automatically pulled out the chair opposite the spectacular view for Clare, which would place her between the two men. Clare decided that sitting next to Max would ruin her composure completely.

Smiling, she complained about a slight draft and asked to switch places with Ham. Max gave her a piercing look as she took her seat across from him, but she glanced toward the fog-shrouded Gulf and pretended not to notice. She must put aside her desires, she told herself, at least until she'd transacted the business at hand.

A waiter appeared at Ham's elbow immediately after they were seated. "Cocktails before dinner?"

"Certainly," Ham said, and turned toward Clare. "What will you have?"

She hesitated and glanced at Max. She'd hoped that the drinking was over for the evening when the men had left the bar. "I'll have a Jack Daniel's and water," she said, and silently dared Max to laugh at her.

"Now that's what I like," Ham said, "a woman who drinks the real stuff. Make that three, unless my buddy Max is ready to quit early?"

"Not me," Max said. "I never turn down J.D. You know that, Ham."

"I've never known you to turn down much of anything," Ham said as the waiter left. He winked at Clare. "Max is a man who knows how to seize an opportunity when it presents itself."

"Really? I'd never have guessed. Max seems so laid-back." Clare gave thanks that the restaurant lights were soft and romantic. Perhaps Durnberg wouldn't be able to gauge her reactions accurately in the dim light. Yes, she knew something about Max's willingness to seize an opportunity, and she'd encouraged him all the way. Now it was time for her to seize some opportunities, too. Business opportunities.

"Oh, I cultivate that laid-back image," Max said, studying her. "Clients like the relaxed approach. But underneath I'm a pretty intense guy."

Clare picked up her water goblet and the ice tinkled against the glass as she brought it unsteadily to her lips. "I would imagine you are," she said and took a long, cooling drink of water.

"Well, you can bring all that intensity to the golf course tomorrow morning. I've reserved an eight-o'clock tee time for the three of us."

"But I don't have my—" Clare began.

"I'll provide clubs," Ham said and glanced up as the waiter brought their drinks. "Thank you, Enrico. We'll order now."

Clare allowed Ham to direct the ordering process. She recognized that he wanted to control their dinner choices as he controlled everything else. Finally the waiter left.

"Here's to the spirit of competition," Ham said, touching his glass to Clare's and then Max's.

Max tipped his glass slightly in Clare's direction and sipped his drink. Over the rim of his glass his gaze was steady.

She shivered, not liking Ham's toast. "Where are we playing golf?" she asked, breaking contact with Max's unwavering gaze. "You don't have a course connected to Sugar Sands."

Ham lifted an eyebrow. "You're right. I don't," he said with some surprise at her knowledge. "But I'm working out an arrangement with the Longboat Key Club.

They'll be delighted to have us play there in the morning. And then, after lunch—" Ham paused as the maître d' approached their table, his attention on Clare.

"Miss Pemberton?" he asked, his body curved slightly in apology for the interruption.

"Yes."

"I'm afraid we have a telephone call for you. The person said it was urgent. Shall I bring one of our cordless phones to the table, or would you prefer to take the call in the lobby?"

Clare frowned. Only two people, her mother and Ron, knew that she was at Sugar Sands. She didn't want either one of them to have urgent reasons to call her. She didn't need more trouble. "I'll take it in the lobby. And thank you," she said, rising as the maître d' held her chair.

"Maybe you should take your drink," Max suggested.

"I don't think—" Then Clare remembered Max's trick of pouring most of it out when he had the chance. For whatever reason, he was still looking out for her welfare. "Perhaps I'll need it, after all," she said and picked up her glass.

The maître d' led her to the lobby area and indicated a phone she could use. After picking up the receiver and identifying herself, Clare waited nervously for the connection. She set her drink down when she realized she'd been unconsciously sipping on it.

"Clare, is that you?"

"Mom? What now?" Clare felt a measure of relief. Ron wouldn't have called for no reason. Her mother would.

"I couldn't leave the office this afternoon without calling you, Clare. The file folders are so dull."

"Mom, I realize office work can be boring sometimes." Clare heard the edge in her tone and softened it. "Maybe you should take a book to read tomorrow."

"Oh, that's not what I meant at all. I have a wonderful idea, and I'm so excited about it I had to tell you. If you want me to, I could start in the morning."

"Start what?" *At least she's called to ask this time,* Clare told herself.

"I want to revamp your filing system."

"Oh, Mom, now wait a—"

"Jazz it up. Give it some character. All those manila folders are so uninteresting, Clare."

"And so inexpensive, Mom. New folders would be a major investment right now. I can't—"

"I found a wonderful bargain when I was out shopping for the plants. Did you get my message about the plants?"

"Yes, Mom." Clare massaged her forehead and debated whether to drink her entire glass of bourbon instead of pouring it out.

"The plants make a big difference, Clare, and if you'd let me improve the looks of your files, too, your office would begin to look like something."

"Maybe you could do a few, and I'll decide when I get back."

"But Clare, the sale on folders will be over. It's a closeout. I have to act now."

Clare made her decision. Tampering with the file folders was less destructive than some things her mother might try. Clare was beginning to understand that her mother's creativity had never had a sufficient outlet, and now that her children were grown and her husband had died, she was running amok.

"So, Clare, what do you think?"

"It's fine, Mom. Just be careful with those files, okay? Be sure not to lose anything or mix up any of the documents. I'm in the process of transferring the information to the computer, but I'm not finished yet."

"Would you like me to do that?"

"No! I mean, that won't be necessary, Mom. Work on the file folders. That'll be great."

"Okay, dear. I'll be in touch."

I'll bet you will, Clare thought. "Good night, Mom." She hung up the phone and stared at her drink. She'd love to down it in one long swallow, but that didn't seem the prudent thing to do considering the evening she had ahead of her.

A quick survey of the lobby produced what she needed, a large rubber plant near the entrance to the restaurant. As she passed the plant she dumped her drink into the potting soil and wondered how bourbon affected growing things. Max hadn't bothered to tell her if he'd killed any plants with this technique.

Max. He was expecting that they'd both pretend extreme exhaustion after dinner, but she was about to break their little pact and take a more aggressive business stance. She wondered if her move would signal the end of his helpful gestures, such as reminding her to get rid of her drink just now.

She couldn't worry about that, she told herself. Max had changed the game by having a drink alone with Ham and quite possibly transacting business. She had a right to alter the game yet again. Pausing until her eyes adjusted to the dimmer light of the restaurant, she walked back to the table where Ham and Max sat.

"Everything okay?" Max said, concern shadowing his features.

"Yes, fine," she said, pushing away a pang of guilt. He was a good man. "It was—" She started to explain about her mother and thought better of it. Ham didn't need to know she had a kooky mother running her agency right now. "It was nothing," she said.

"Urgent phone calls usually are," Ham said, dismissing the matter. "People overuse the word urgent. I believe we were talking about tomorrow's schedule when you left. After lunch I've planned my grudge match with Max the Magnificent, here, on the tennis court. Perhaps you'd like to watch?"

"I wouldn't miss it." Clare found that she couldn't meet Max's gaze often. The lurching in her stomach each time she did was too distracting.

"After that I thought we'd do some Windsurfing if the breeze is good. Ever been Windsurfing, Clare?"

"No. I've never been surfing at all."

"Max can teach you. Right, Max? Soon you'll be good enough that we can set up some races. Max knows all about surfing, and all about surfers, for that matter."

"Watch yourself, Ham, old buddy."

Clare glanced at Max and caught her breath at the flash of red-hot anger in his eyes. Something about surfing or surfers was a charged subject for Max, and Ham knew it. He'd deliberately baited Max again.

"Sounds like a full day," Clare said, more to ease the tension at the table than anything else. Yet here was her perfect opening and she decided to take it. "Perhaps the thing to do, Ham, is schedule an appointment with me after dinner tonight, so that we can go over my program before we launch into all those activities." Without looking at him she could sense Max's bewilderment. "That way," she rushed on, "you'll have a chance to think about my proposal, mull it over in between golf shots or tennis games."

"Well, now." Ham looked from her to Max and back again. "You've caught me off guard here. A little combo plays dance music beginning about eight, and I'd thought the two of you would want to take advantage of that."

"I'd feel better if we went over this proposal, Ham," Clare said, focusing on him and trying to block Max out of her mind. "It's what I'm here for, after all."

"Uh, yes, of course." Ham glanced at her. "But you don't seem to have brought any materials with you, unless you have hidden pockets in that bewitching dress of yours."

"I wouldn't doubt it," Max said. "She's pretty clever."

"I left my briefcase at the front desk. After dinner it would be no trouble to slip into your office and go over everything. I think it's the best plan."

Ham took a drink of bourbon and narrowed his eyes, as if considering all the angles of Clare's suggestion. "All right," he said at last. "Although I hate to take away Max's dancing partner."

"I can wait, have another drink in the bar, until your discussion is finished," Max said evenly. "I'm certainly not ready for bed, and dancing might be a nice idea. What do you think, Clare?"

She couldn't read his expression. "It might be fun," she said, on uncertain ground with these new plans. If she begged off and said she'd be too tired, it would sound very much like their original plot to be alone. Now she wasn't sure if any of it was a good idea, the dancing or the dangerous alternative of returning to the cottage.

This attraction became more filled with land mines every minute. This afternoon she'd wanted to believe that she and Max could be competitors and lovers at the same time. Tonight the reality of the situation was making her doubt it. She couldn't speak for Max, but as for her, if the choice came down to business or pleasure, she'd have to choose business.

"Then it's settled," Ham said. "Clare and I will take a few minutes after dinner to discuss her program, and after that we can all relax and enjoy ourselves."

"Sounds fine to me," Max said and polished off his drink. Clare hadn't seen him pour a drop of this one in a potted plant.

The meal was excellent, but Clare ate it more for something to do than out of hunger. True to Max's prediction, a ceremony took place at seven-thirty to award a prize for the best seashell found that day. Ham confided to Clare and Max that he had the best shell collection on the island and could have won the contest dozens of times if he'd chosen to enter. Clare wondered when, in his frantic competitive schedule, Ham found time to comb the beach for shells.

For a while Max and Ham discussed tennis, and Clare was relieved of carrying her share of the conversation. She disciplined her thoughts to include only the proposal she would present soon. Beyond that point were treacherous waters that she didn't feel prepared to navigate.

"You know, Clare, I don't recall that you mentioned having a business associate in Sarasota." Ham had moved from bourbon to wine during the meal. He refilled his goblet and topped off Clare's.

"I wasn't sure if there'd be time to see him," she replied, wishing Ham would drop the subject.

"Have you been working together long?"

"Not long, no."

Ham pushed his empty plate away. "Very interesting," he said, patting his mouth with his folded napkin.

Clare glanced at Max, who knew that this "business associate" had once been her fiancé. How was he interpreting her reluctance to discuss Ron? Clare saw it as good business sense, but Max might wonder if she and Ron had rekindled the flame after seeing each other again. Clare's head began to ache. Paradise wasn't all it was cracked up to be.

"Dessert, anyone? Or an after-dinner liqueur?" Ham asked, signaling a waiter.

"No thanks." Max pushed back his chair. "If you two will excuse me, I think I'll take a walk along the beach and work off some of that great food."

Clare had the insane urge to leap up and go with him. But of course she couldn't.

"A walk after dinner," Ham said, shaking his head. "You must be getting old, Max. You used to match me brandy for brandy."

"Yeah, well, I read this article that said walking is good for the heart. Walking on the beach is even better. I've started thinking about my heart recently." Max looked directly at Clare.

"My God, Max. I never thought I'd see the day when hard-living, hard-drinking Armstrong became concerned about his health."

Max clapped Durnberg on the shoulder. "I don't expect you to understand, old buddy. And Clare's too young to sympathize. She's still got the world to conquer."

Regret twisted inside Clare. More than anything, Max was hurt by her rejection of their earlier plan to pretend fatigue and turn in early, and she didn't enjoy hurting him. Yet didn't she have the right to pursue her goals, just as he was pursuing his? She was number two in this race; she had to work harder. Max had assumed that she couldn't win and possibly expected her to give up and spend all her time with him, instead. She couldn't do that.

"I'll be in the bar, when you two have finished your discussion," Max said, glancing at Clare.

"Fine." She smiled at him. No matter what happened, they still could be civilized and friendly about it. While she danced with him she could point out that he'd used his time with Ham to good advantage and she had to do the same. She could also suggest that a love affair between them was a romantic but unworkable idea.

After Max was out of earshot, Ham leaned toward her. "I think he's smitten by you."

"Don't be ridiculous," she said and willed herself not to blush.

"There's nothing ridiculous about it. Unless you consider him too old for you?"

"Of course not!" she blurted before she could think.

"Ah." Ham leaned back in his chair and folded his hands over his slim stomach as he watched her with the eyes of a stalking animal.

Clare put her napkin beside her plate and gazed at him with as cool a look as she could muster. "Why don't I get my briefcase and meet you in your office in five minutes?"

He didn't change position. "That would be fine."

Clare wanted to issue a ringing denial of any feelings between her and Max, but she knew that doing so would only confirm Durnberg's gleeful suspicions. She pushed back her chair.

"Here. Allow me." Durnberg seemed to uncoil his body as he stood, which accentuated his predatory look as he helped her out of her chair. "Do you know where my office is?"

"They can direct me at the front desk."

"Of course. You're a resourceful young woman."

"Thank you for the meal, Ham. It was delicious."

"My pleasure."

She hurried from the restaurant and fought the desire to run onto the beach in search of Max. Without him, she didn't feel completely safe. Unfortunately she didn't feel completely safe with him, either, but for different reasons.

Moments later she was gazing at Durnberg across the uncluttered surface of a massive desk. This office, too, contained a trophy case full of awards and Durnberg's touted shell collection.

"Am I to assume you're licensed in Florida, then?" Ham said immediately after she'd settled herself.

"Yes." She noticed a new interest in Durnberg's cool gray eyes. "I'm prepared to quote you a rate for insuring both Flagstaff Fairways and Sugar Sands."

"Hmm." He leaned back in his chair and studied her. "In that case I want to know more about your associate, who would undoubtedly be handling things on this end. Was that him on the phone?"

Clare realized that Durnberg hadn't dismissed the phone call after all. He'd simply waited until he could grill her more thoroughly. "No, that wasn't Ron," she said, determined not to give away more information than necessary.

"I see." He waited, and when she said nothing more, he leaned forward. "Then tell me about Ron."

"Ron Trilling is an excellent agent. I've known him since we went to Northern Arizona University together. If you decide in favor of my program, he'll do a fine job for you here in Florida."

"Ah, so he's a classmate of yours." Durnberg's eyes glittered. "Were you two ever romantically involved?"

Clare gripped the briefcase in her lap. "I don't understand why that's pertinent," she said carefully.

"It is if you want me to consider your program. I find that romantic entanglements can make business matters, shall we say, sticky? And I have a second reason for knowing, a personal one. I don't want you leading my old buddy Max down the primrose path if you have an interest in another man."

Furious, Clare half rose from her chair. Her first instinct was to leave the company of this miserable man at once. The business wasn't worth it.

"Now, now," Durnberg said, waving her back down again. "That's all I needed to know. Your reaction tells me well enough that you care about Max Armstrong or you wouldn't be so angry. I could tell Max was a bit worried about this Ron person, but now I see that he has no need to be."

"Ham," she said, fighting to keep her tone even. "I'd appreciate it if we kept personalities out of this. I have an excellent program for you, and if you take it, I will service your account to the best of my ability. Ron will handle anything that needs on-site attention here in Florida. I'd like to leave Max and my private life out of the discussion, if you don't mind."

Durnberg showed his even teeth. "What a spoil-sport."

"I have some printouts for you to look at," Clare said, unsnapping her briefcase. "You'll notice that my program is inclusive, which is my chief selling point. Right now the Armstrong Agency handles only the casualty portion of your coverage. I'd like to be your agent for everything, including your health and life insurance plans." She spread her material in front of him.

His smile, which conveyed malice more than humor, widened. "You're ready to put a whole lot of folks out of business, aren't you?"

"That's not my concern. My concern is for you, the client. You deserve the simplicity of a single phone call when problems arise. A man with your responsibilities shouldn't have to keep track of which agent is involved with which policy."

"Does Max have any idea what you're up to?"

"I'd appreciate it if we didn't discuss Max except as necessary to an evaluation of your present coverage."

Durnberg shook his head. "My, my."

"And in reference to that, I promise to update your portfolio annually and change insurance carriers whenever it would be beneficial to you. I don't believe the Armstrong Agency is doing that." Clare found that by referring to the agency and not the man, she could pretend she wasn't criticizing Max himself. How she wished that Max had turned out to be the brash, pushy man she'd first envisioned.

Durnberg gave his attention to the sheets in front of him. "No, Max hasn't changed carriers in several years. Are you saying that he's been lazy?"

"Perhaps inattentive is a better word," Clare said, swallowing the distaste in her mouth.

"Well, his ex has been giving him a hard time. Before the divorce she was complaining that he spent too much time on his work. But then when he tried to reverse the trend, it was too late; they'd already grown too far apart."

Clare didn't want to hear it. She suspected Durnberg of stirring up sympathy for Max to further complicate an already complicated matter. Anyone else listening to Durnberg would believe that he was Max's true friend, but Clare had witnessed the jealousy and heard the pointed jibes. E. Hamilton Durnberg had no real interest in Max except to humiliate him. Unfortunately, Clare could help Durnberg do just that.

She noticed that he'd become absorbed in the computer printouts. She'd surprised him, apparently, with her proposal to handle all of his insurance needs. Both he and Max had underestimated her from the beginning, and she took some pride in Durnberg's interest now. "Do you have any questions or would you prefer I go over each section first?"

He looked up as if he'd forgotten that she was there. "What? Oh, no questions at the moment, Clare, but I'll certainly have a few when I've finished reviewing your figures. Tell you what. Why don't you run along and meet Max and let me have some time with this proposal?"

She gritted her teeth. Apparently he enjoyed telling people to "run along." She snapped her briefcase closed again and stood. "All right," she said. "Feel free to ask me anything you like about the program. At any time."

"At any time?" He winked. "I wouldn't dream of taking you literally on that."

"Well, you can," she said, lifting her chin.

"Go meet Max," he said, waving her off. "And I'll send Santiago for the two of you at seven in the morning. Have a pleasant evening."

"You won't be joining us for the dancing?" Clare had expected, even hoped for, Durnberg's presence as a chaperone, despite her dislike for him.

"God, no. Dancing bores me to tears."

Clare understood at once. Dancing was cooperative rather than competitive. Unless, of course, a man used dancing to compete for a woman, and Durnberg had shown no signs of wanting to compete with Max for her.

She realized that she knew almost nothing about Durnberg's personal life, although he spent a great deal of energy prying into that of others. She doubted that he was currently married or had any children. Neither this office nor the other one had contained any framed photographs of family members.

"I guess I'll see you in the morning," she said, glancing at him, but he'd already returned his attention to the papers in front of him and she left without saying anything more. She had a chance, she thought, a real chance. Winning the account had seemed like a dream until now, but Durnberg obviously was interested in what she'd given him.

She wanted to twirl around in the lobby and shout with excitement, but instead she crossed to the front desk and quietly asked the uniformed clerk to store her briefcase until morning.

A few steps away was the entrance to the lounge, where Max would be waiting. She hesitated, while wild plans of returning to her cottage and locking all the doors swirled through her mind. He would get that message loud and clear, and perhaps it was the best message she could send under the circumstances.

But it was also the coward's way out, and Clare couldn't take it. She'd meet him as they'd arranged, she decided, and dance at least once with him. During that time she'd explain that this afternoon had been a mistake and that the best thing for both of them would be to maintain a distant yet friendly relationship.

She found him, his back toward her, on a stool at the bar. She remembered what that broad, muscular back looked like unclothed, and her throat grew dry. *No*, she lectured herself, *don't want him.*

She walked quickly to the bar and slid onto the stool beside him. "What're you drinking, mister?" she asked, glancing at the colorless liquid in his glass.

He turned, and his gaze was disturbingly steady. "Water," he said. "Want some?"

"Sure." Her heart was thumping, just from that look that seemed to reach inside her and grab hold. No matter how she talked to herself, she couldn't manage to put distance between herself and this man.

Max turned and signaled to the bartender. "Could we have another of your H_2O specials for the lady, John?"

The bartender smiled. "You bet."

"So," Max returned his attention to her. "Everything all taken care of?"

"Max, I know you didn't expect me to set up that meeting, but after all, you had time alone with Durnberg before dinner. I saw you writing figures on a napkin and I assume you were quoting some new rates. I deserve an equal chance."

He laughed. "I probably should have been quoting him some new rates."

"You weren't?"

"I was writing down the point spread for our bet on Sunday's game between the Dolphins and the Bears."

"Oh." Her water arrived and she drank it while she collected her thoughts. Max hadn't been using his opportunity to discuss business with Durnberg, but so what? That only meant that he was so certain of himself that he hadn't thought it necessary. Well, soon he'd know that he'd been wrong to be so complacent.

Max pushed his glass aside. "Ready for that dance?"

She realized that she didn't have to dance with him in order to say her piece. And from the way his presence was already affecting her, she'd be better off out of his arms, not in them. "Max, I think perhaps I allowed the circumstances and the beautiful setting to go to my head this afternoon," she said, not looking at him.

"I know you do," he said quietly. "Now how about that dance?"

"That's what I'm trying to say." She glanced into his eyes and wished she hadn't. "We'll both be much better off if we keep our relationship . . . platonic."

He smiled the slow, sensuous smile that tore her apart. "I only asked for a dance, Clare. Surely Joel's sister isn't the sort of person who makes a promise and then breaks it."

She put her hand on his arm, pleading with him. "You're not going to force me to honor that promise, are you, Max?"

His gaze moved over her face and flickered downward, taking in the evidence of her discomfort in her rapid breathing and flushed skin. "Yes," he said, looking directly into her eyes, "I certainly am."

8

CLARE BEGAN LOSING the fight from the moment Max drew her into his arms on the dance floor. The music had a Latin flavor that teased her hips into a sensuous rhythm as she followed Max's smooth lead. She vaguely remembered something called a rumba and decided this was a rumba. She hadn't realized what a potent dance it could be.

Max held her close, but not tight. Enough space remained between them to create a tantalizing friction that was more erotic than if he'd crushed her to his chest. His persuasive movements flowed around her, guiding her as surely as a river current carries a leaf. She fought the urge to nestle her cheek against his shoulder and abandon all her misgivings. His fluid motion on the dance floor suggested his ease and control as a lover, and longing settled deep within her.

His voice rumbled in her ear. "What changed your mind about tonight?"

Her heart ached as she gazed over his shoulder at the revolving kaleidoscope of couples on the dance floor. "I had a chance to think, that's all."

"About your friend Ron?"

"Ron has nothing to do with this."

"Couldn't prove it by me. Before you left with him you were melting like butter in my arms. When you came back it was business as usual, complete with phone calls in the middle of dinner." He executed a spin that left her dizzy.

"That was my mother again," she said, clutching his shoulder for support. Beneath the material of his Western sports jacket his muscles flexed, reminding her of the pleasure of caressing his bare shoulder. She consciously relaxed her grip.

"Your mother? No kidding."

"No kidding, and by the way, thanks for suggesting that I take my drink to the phone with me. I used it to water the rubber plant."

His arm tensed, drawing her imperceptibly closer. "I probably should have let you drink it."

"So I wouldn't make as effective a presentation to Durnberg?" she asked, her tone sharpened by her increased awareness of him and the lure of his body.

Without warning he brought her in snug against him and put his lips to her ear. "I don't give a damn about your presentation to Durnberg."

Clare stumbled at the shock of the intimate contact but he held her steady in his iron grip and they resumed the smooth rhythm of the dance. "Then you wanted me mellow for your own purposes," she said, struggling to remain rational as his heat drugged her senses.

"Would've been nice." He rubbed the small of her back as they danced.

Clare panicked as desire for him threatened to overcome reason. She had to say something, anything, to break the spell. "Is that how you like your women, tipsy and compliant?" she asked.

His body against hers became rigid and finally his breath hissed out against her ear. "You win," he said, and relaxed his hold on her. The music stopped and he moved away.

She'd gotten what she wanted. He wouldn't pursue her anymore, she knew. Max was aggressive in his passion, but he wasn't a bully. Unfortunately that knowledge made her want him even more. After forsaking the shelter of his arms, she felt alone and bereft.

"What's your pleasure, Clare?" he asked as the band started into a faster number. "You call it."

She took a deep breath. "Max, I apologize for that last remark. It was rude. I think we're both overtired and need some rest. I'd like you to walk me home, if you don't mind."

He nodded, his expression carefully guarded. "Do you have a coat?"

"I left it at the desk."

He held out his hand. "Claim check?"

She reached into the skirt pocket of her dress and gave it to him.

"I'll be right back. We can go out through those French doors and walk back on the beach, if you're up to it."

Sorrow at what was lost softened her answer. "I'd like that," she said. She watched him walk away with his self-assured carriage. Instinctively she'd known how to hurt him, by striking at his pride. Max Armstrong didn't need liquor to lure women into bed; she of all people realized that.

But now that she'd created a distance between them, she dared not eliminate it. Her body still pulsed from their dance together. Because of this strong attraction to Max, she'd almost missed her chance tonight to present her program to Durnberg. She mustn't forget that lesson.

He reappeared with her coat over his arm. As he wound his way past tables sprinkled with late diners, several women glanced up at him. Clare couldn't blame them. She wished that for one night she could be someone else, someone free to love him without fear of the consequences to her future and that of her family.

He draped her coat over her shoulders and his hands lingered for a moment. "Maybe it was the dim light, but you looked almost friendly as I was walking back."

Willing to eliminate the hostility, she turned to face him. "I am friendly. Remember when you suggested that we could be just that? Friends?"

He smiled and guided her toward the doors leading to the beach. "Yeah. I didn't mean it."

"But—"

"Or rather, I meant the part about keeping our personal and business lives separate." He paused before opening the door for her. "But friends? Come on, Clare . . . you're young, but you can't be that naive."

She gazed into his eyes. No, she wasn't that naive. She'd known from the beginning that the word *friends* was a convenient ruse. "Maybe that's my problem," she said as Max opened the door and she stepped onto the bricked terrace. "I'm too young. I'm not sophisticated enough. A woman with more experience would be able to manage her affairs, business and otherwise, without getting confused."

"Maybe." He cupped her elbow as they walked down brick stairs to the sand. "Want to take off your shoes? I can manage, but with those heels you're going to sink in at every step. I didn't think of that."

"I'll take off the shoes. Of course the nylons will be ruined if I do."

He glanced at her. "Once we're out of range of these spotlights you can take off the nylons, too, as far as I'm concerned. I promise it won't turn me into a crazed creature of lust."

She smiled at him as she leaned on the stair railing and pulled off her shoes. "I like you, Max. Darn it, I wish we were two strangers who had happened to meet here on vacation."

"We could be," he said gently, watching her with his hands in the pockets of his slacks. "That's, in a way, what I've been suggesting, what I thought you understood until tonight. We don't have to be bound by who we are, unless you insist on it."

She gazed at him, captivated. "You mean pretend we're different people?"

"I don't think we have to pretend. I think with each other we would be different people."

She sensed danger, yet she couldn't silence him with a change of subject. "I don't . . . know that I understand."

He angled his head down the beach. "Let's walk."

"Okay."

He made no effort to hold her hand as they scrunched side by side through clean, perfect sand. Real beaches, she thought, were littered with broken shells and seaweed. So much of this trip to Florida hadn't seemed real. She wondered if that, more than anything, had seduced her into wanting what she shouldn't want.

After they'd walked in silence for several yards Max began speaking. "A lady I used to know once accused me of missing the moment at hand because I was always worried about the next one coming up," he said slowly.

Clare guessed that the woman might be his ex-wife. "Yes, but sometimes you have to think ahead, Max."

"Think ahead, yes. But worry? You can give that a pass and never miss it. I've learned that the hard way."

"You think I shouldn't worry about the effect our relationship might have on my chances of getting Durnberg's business?"

"That's right. I think you should respond to the moment, be the person you want to be at that moment. If it's a shrewd businesswoman, fine. It it's a sensuous lover, great. You don't have to be the same all the time, Clare. No one is. And one facet of you doesn't have to control the other. You can be everything you want to be."

Clare took a deep breath. The moist, salty air made her feel reckless, not cautious, but she tried to keep logic close at hand, nonetheless. "I just think, Max, that life would be simpler if we didn't add a sexual element to our present situation."

"Ah, simplicity. What about richness? What about excitement?"

"Max, you know how you affect me, but—"

"No, I don't," he said quietly. "I'm only guessing."

"Well, you're guessing right," she confessed, wondering if that was the wisest thing to say. Probably not. "But I—well, shoot."

"What's the matter?" He stopped when she did.

"My toe just went through the end of my stocking. It doesn't really matter except it feels funny to walk like that."

"So, take them off. We're way beyond the spotlights."

"Yeah, I think I will." She put down her shoes.

"Want me to look away?"

"I don't know why. This coat hangs down to my knees. I could get totally undressed using it as a shield and nobody would know."

"Oh, Clare, you do have a way with words."

"Sorry." She turned slightly so that her coat covered her activity and reached under her dress for the fasteners on her garter belt. Then she peeled the nylon off, tucked it in her shoe, and repeated the process on the other leg. "All set," she said, picking up her shoes and turning back to Max.

He swallowed. "I thought . . . everyone went in for panty hose these days."

"Not everyone," she said, transfixed by the desire that roughened his statement. "Max, I didn't really mean to—"

"The hell you didn't."

"You're the one who suggested I take them off," she protested, "the one who said he wouldn't turn into a crazed creature of lust if I did."

"I thought it would be panty hose."

"Why didn't you ask? Why didn't you qualify your suggestion with 'unless you have on a garter belt, which *will* turn me into a crazed creature of lust'?"

"God." In two strides he'd bridged the distance between them and swept her into his arms with a force that knocked the shoes from her hand and dislodged her coat from her shoulders. "My big mistake has been trying to talk to you. I know what you want and so do you."

"Max, I—" His mouth silenced whatever she'd intended to say, and as his lips moved insistently against hers, she forgot what it might have been. With a moan of surrender she welcomed the defiant thrust of his tongue. He poured his frustration into the kiss, and she answered with a blaze of passion that left her trembling in his arms when at last he raised his head.

His voice was hoarse. "There. Is it settled, finally?"

She had no resistance left. "Yes," she whispered.

"We're almost home," he said releasing her to reach for her scattered shoes and crumpled coat. He carried them in one hand and held out the other. "Let's go."

She hurried with him through the sand and onto the deck of her cottage. "The key's in my coat pocket," she said, and Max let go of her hand to unlock the door.

The lights that Max had left on greeted them as they stepped inside. He locked the door behind them and closed the drapes. Then he tossed the keys on an end table and turned toward her. "Clare, you look frightened again," he said, stripping off his tie and unbuttoning his collar as he crossed to where she stood.

"When you're holding me, everything seems so right. But when you're not, I wonder what on earth I'm doing."

"I think we can fix that." He cradled her face between his cupped hands and gazed into her eyes. "Because I'm going to hold you all night long."

Anticipation beat through her veins at the promise in his golden eyes. "How will we ever make it through Durnberg's schedule tomorrow?" she asked, fingering the lapels of his sport coat.

He smiled and rubbed her cheeks with his thumbs. "I'm not going to worry about that in advance. How about you?"

Drawing strength from his strength, she grew bold and eased the sport coat from his shoulders. "Maybe . . . maybe I'll need some help, to stop me from worrying."

He threw the discarded coat in the general direction of a chair. "I'll see what I can do about it," he said, scooping her up in his arms.

"Max, for goodness sakes." Clare started to laugh. "You make me feel like Scarlett O'Hara."

"Then we're even," he said, carrying her through the bedroom doorway, "because you make me feel like Rhett Butler."

"And now what happens?" she asked, winding her arms around his neck and gazing into his eyes.

"As if you didn't know," he said, settling her on the bed and leaning down to nibble the soft skin of her throat. "You, the lady who was prowling around in my bathroom in her underwear, checking my supplies." His kisses moved lower to the neckline of her dress as he reached beneath her and found the top of the garment's zipper.

"Max . . . I hope you don't think . . ." Then she sighed as he pulled the dress and the straps of her bra down over her shoulders and began kissing her bared breasts.

"I think you're beautiful, that's what I think."

"But I don't usually—" She arched toward him as his tongue circled her nipple.

"I didn't think you did," he murmured, just before he took her into his mouth.

Finished with doubting, she closed her eyes and gave herself up to pure sensation without thought—the smoothness of his tongue across her nipple, the ridge of his teeth, the roughness of his beard rubbing her breast, the feathered brush of his open shirt collar. She caressed the curve of his ears and tangled her fingers in his hair as he drew passion from her in dazzling amounts.

Gently he pulled away, leaving her breasts moist and throbbing, and she opened her eyes to find him gazing down at her, his expression full of an emotion that she dared not name. She imagined his eyes reflected what she felt, too, and she was frightened again.

"No," he murmured. "It's okay."

Her tongue was thick, unworkable. "I . . . I didn't expect . . . to feel so . . ."

"Nobody ever does," he said softly. "That's the thing about miracles."

Still staring into his eyes, she reached for the buttons of his shirt. He let her undo them without interruption and held her gaze when she placed both hands on his bare chest. His heart thudded against the palm of her right hand and she gloried in the strength of its beat.

"You know," he said, combing a lock of hair back from her cheek, "lust is wonderful, but love is much better."

"It doesn't make sense," she said, caressing him, treasuring the warmth of his skin. "We couldn't possibly be in—"

"No," he said, cupping her breast and watching her face as he stroked her. "Of course not."

She trembled and reached up to pull him down to her waiting lips. "Of course not," she whispered, kissing him hungrily and pushing away his shirt to press her aching breasts against his bare skin.

He lifted himself away enough to tug her dress over her hips. "Forgive me if I'm ruining your dress," he whispered against her mouth.

"Nothing matters." She kissed his jaw, his cheeks, the lobes of his ears as she peeled off his shirt. "Please take this away," she said between kisses. "Take everything away and come to bed with me."

Without a word he left the bed and walked into her bathroom.

"In the drawer," she said, knowing what he was after.

He returned and placed the box on the bedside table. Clare had expected some embarrassment with this man she'd known for such a short time, but there was none. Instead, the presence of the box on the nightstand was a promise of what was ahead for them.

Her gaze left the box and returned to the man who had brought it. He'd taken off his boots and socks and now stood a few feet from her, regarding her with a concentration that made her shiver. She pulsed with excitement as he reached for his belt buckle.

Earlier tonight that buckle had pressed against her stomach when he'd become angry and crushed her in his arms on the dance floor. She remembered how the oval impression of it had felt through her dress, and she remembered something else from that encounter—a demanding hardness between his thighs. She'd denied knowledge of his arousal to herself then, believing that to confront his needs would be to expose her own.

Now she waited, mouth dry, as he pulled the belt through the loops and tossed it to the carpeted floor. The rasp of his zipper sent chills up her spine, and within seconds he stood before her clad only in briefs that barely contained his swelling manhood.

"The rest," she murmured and enjoyed every second of his final strip. He was magnificent, as she'd known he would be, and she wanted him with a possessive fierceness that amazed her. Without waiting for him to come to her, she got up from the bed. Looking directly into his eyes, she walked the short distance until they barely touched—the tip of her breasts to his chest and his manhood against the silken surface of her half slip.

"I guess the reluctant maiden has disappeared," he said, his voice gravelly.

"You said I could be whoever I wanted to be."

He swallowed. "You're a tease."

"So are you," she whispered.

"I just followed instructions."

"Would you like some more?" she asked, inching forward until her nipples flattened against his chest.

He cupped her silk-covered bottom and urged her another step closer. "I think it's my turn for instructions," he said, rubbing the swell of her buttocks. "Lord, but I love the feel of this material." He slipped both hands beneath the elastic of her slip and panties. "And what's under it," he added, his breathing more uneven as he caressed her.

"Is that an instruction?"

"No. I'll take care of this." He slid the garments over her hips and bent to push them past her knees until they fell in a heap on the carpet. "Now," he said, reaching for her again.

She moved out of reach. "It seems," she said, her heart beating rapidly at her audacity, "that you have no gift for giving instructions. You haven't issued a single one, so I'll have to imagine what you'd like."

He looked puzzled as she smiled and approached him again. Then she took his hands in hers and very slowly sank to her knees in front of him.

"I'll imagine that you'd like me to love you," she said, releasing his hands to caress him. "All of you."

"Clare . . . God . . ." His moan of pleasure spiked her excitement as she leaned forward and tasted his passion. He'd been right. With him, she was a different person, a daring, impetuous woman who made a gift of her sexuality to the man who stirred her to the depths of her being.

She loved him until his legs shook and he urged her to her feet. When she gazed into his eyes, she knew that he would never forget her. Whatever happened between them, this moment would be a part of their lives forever.

His kiss was deep, as if he were pledging something that couldn't be expressed in words. Then silently he led her to the bed and threw back the covers. She stretched out on the smooth sheets and gazed up at him.

"I don't want to use these," he said, picking up the box on the table and opening it. "Every instinct tells me to destroy all barriers between us."

"I know," she said softly.

"But I will use them, Clare." His golden gaze swept over her. "I won't put you at risk."

"Nor I, you," she said, knowing that she'd never want to place a man under that kind of unplanned obligation. She and Max had no idea what the future held for them. So many things could happen to trample the tenderness they'd found with each other. Clare closed her eyes and made a silent wish that the special emotion they felt tonight would survive, somehow.

She felt his weight on the mattress next to her and his lips brushing her eyelids. She opened her eyes and gazed into his face as he stroked her cheek with the flat of his hand. She waited, trembling. He caressed the curve of her jaw and the hollow of her throat before gliding his palm over the peak of each breast. She imagined he was creating her, and each movement was a brush stroke that highlighted a part of her body that had never existed quite this way before.

His fingers followed the curve of her ribcage and his thumb dipped into the hollow of her navel. She held her breath, but he skipped past the heated core of her and traced the line of her instep, the swell of her calf, the secret place behind her knee. At last he traveled up the slope of her thigh and returned to the spot that ached for his touch.

Pressing the heel of his hand gently against the moist blond triangle, he affirmed the essence of her desire with a penetrating touch that made her writhe and call his name.

"I'm here," he whispered, moving over her. "And I need you every bit as much."

Clare knew that if he didn't fill her now and take away the wonderful, unbearable ache of wanting him, that she would go crazy. She grasped his hips and lifted her own. When he pushed forward, so did she, and their coming together wrung a cry from each of them.

She thought briefly of the dance floor as he guided the rhythm with a sureness that left her free to experience the glorious response of her body to his. Her skin flushed in celebration; her heart beat to a song of deliverance as he took her past the scanty pleasures she'd known before to a rich feast of sensation.

"Oh, Max," she cried softly. "Max, it's so good."

"It gets better," he said, panting now. "Go with it, Clare."

"I am," she moaned. "Max . . . Max!" She arched upward as the splendor overtook her at last. She heard his companion cry with a sense of wonder, for his shout of joy was a perfect echo of her own.

9

AFTER THEY BOTH grew still Max lay quietly, making sure he didn't rest his full weight on Clare's damp body. He was afraid if he moved or spoke, he'd wake up and discover that none of this had happened, that it was some sort of middle-aged fantasy.

But God, he didn't feel middle-aged. He felt vibrant and alive, eager for the next moment, because Clare would be part of it. He felt . . . like a man in love. After the bleak desert his life had resembled lately, finding this golden woman was like stumbling on a secret oasis. He prayed that she wasn't a mirage that would disappear when he kept the Flagstaff Fairways account and she came away with nothing.

She stirred beneath him and he lifted his head. He willed her to open her eyes so that he could plumb the depths of her green gaze and discover himself there. He wanted to trust this gut feeling, but he needed to see her eyes again.

Her lashes fluttered. He noticed a touch of mascara and the faint smudge of pale green eyeshadow. Her lipstick was gone, kissed away by their passion. He thought of how he'd love to lean in the doorway of a shared bathroom and watch her stroke the shadow over her eyelids and brush on the mascara with quick movements of her wrist. He pictured the way she'd bend toward the mirror so that the top of her dress would gape just enough for him to glimpse the valley between her breasts.

Slowly she opened her eyes. "Hi," she said, her voice husky.

"Hi yourself." *Yes,* he thought, rejoicing. *I wasn't imagining anything. She feels what I feel.* Her smile appeared, and he kissed the faint indentation of the dimple in her cheek. "Promise not to go away? I have a little matter to take care of."

"I promise."

He eased away from her. Damn the nuisance of birth control, he thought, heading for the bathroom. He hadn't minded so much with the two brief affairs he'd had following his divorce, because he'd known the relationships weren't going anywhere and a pregnancy would have been out of the question.

But from the first kiss he'd known that Clare was different. With her he longed to share the carefree fun of making love first thing in the morning before either of them got out of bed, or making love at night, falling nearly asleep still joined and waking to love again, almost without changing position. He could have done it a moment ago with ease, but it wasn't practical.

When he returned to the bedroom she'd pulled the sheet over her and was lying on her side with her hand tucked under her cheek and her eyes wide and distant. He frowned. She was thinking again.

He stood by the bed and gazed down at her. "Cold? Or modest?"

"Thinking."

"I figured." He sat on the bed and stroked her hair. "That can get you into trouble."

Her dimple flashed. "And what we just did can't?"

"Not unless Ham rigged these things." He held up the open box.

She sat up, immediately, clutching the sheet over her breasts. "Max! Do you think he'd—"

"No, no," he said, chuckling as he took her gently by the shoulders and rubbed her soft skin. "I'm sorry. I didn't mean to scare you to death. The box wasn't opened. The packages aren't opened. Besides, Ham's not that diabolical."

"I sometimes wonder. Earlier tonight, after you left for your walk, I had the strangest feeling that he was some sort of predatory snake."

"In the Garden of Eden?" Max asked, kissing her bare shoulder.

"Maybe. And we sure took a big bite of the apple."

He pushed aside her hair, damp at the roots, and ran his tongue along the curve of her neck. "Then we might as well finish it off," he murmured, tasting salt on her skin and breathing the mingled fragrances of cologne and sweat, both hers and his. In the restaurant she'd had an untouched beauty that stirred and challenged him, but the tumbled, mussed look of her now drove him wild.

"I'll be an open book tomorrow," she said, sighing as he slowly tugged the sheet from her grasp. "Durnberg will know everything after one look at my face."

He nuzzled the hollow of her throat as he stroked the tension from her spine. Gradually he felt her relax. "Do you think he'll be able to tell exactly how many times we made love by looking at your face?"

"Now, Max," she said, her tongue growing languid, "you're being silly."

"No, logical." He drew the sheet away and guided her to the rumpled pillows. Then he allowed himself a leisurely visual trip from her tousled blond hair to her pink-tipped toenails. She was rosy and ready for more. At last he gazed into her green eyes and discovered passion building there again. "If your face will look the same, whether I make love to you once or more than once, then I vote for more than once."

Her slow smile and half-lowered eyelashes sent the blood racing through his system. He trembled with passion he hadn't thought himself capable of feeling. Oh, he would make love to her more than once, all right. He would love her until he'd learned every secret place on her soft body. He would love her until she'd whispered the secret fantasies that she'd never told another man. In the hours left to them before dawn he would fill the hushed quiet of this room with her ardent cries . . . and his.

CLARE WOKE to the sound of whistling in the shower, her shower. Raising up on one elbow, she took inventory of the chaos around her. The sheets were hopelessly twisted and flung to the end of the bed. The bedspread was on the floor, along with one pillow. She suspected that her dress and bra were tangled together somewhere under the bedspread.

Beside the bed her slip and panties lay in an abandoned jumble, and the rest of the room was strewn with Max's clothes. His belt formed an S next to the chair where he'd tossed his slacks, his shirt hung by one sleeve over the doorknob and his briefs had landed on the edge of the wastebasket. Clare flopped back down and stared at the ceiling, which was about the only part of the room left untouched by their romp last night.

And a romp it had been, she thought, smiling even as she wondered how on earth they'd disguise this mayhem from the resort staff. Durnberg might have spies among the maids, for all she knew.

The shower stopped but the whistling didn't. She stretched languidly and thought how nice it would be to stay in bed all day. She couldn't understand Max's energy, considering that they'd had almost no sleep and quite a bit of activity.

"Rise and shine!" He stood in the bathroom doorway with one towel around his hips while he used a second one to dry his hair.

"Oh, Lord," she groaned, sitting up. "Are you a morning person?"

He stopped toweling his hair and looked offended. "I don't know how you can imply such a thing. I'd say that I function perfectly well at night, considering all the times that we—"

"Okay," she said, laughing, both at his defense of himself and the tousled condition of his hair. She could see the little boy that Max Armstrong once had been. "I meant, are you always this cheerful in the morning?"

"No," he said, looping the towel around his neck and walking over to her. "But after last night, you may never be able to wipe the grin off my face."

She took the ends of the towel around his neck and used them to pull herself to her knees on the bed in front of him. He smelled of soap and shampoo . . . and Max. "Last night was beautiful," she said. "No matter what happens, I'll never forget it."

"Hey." He tweaked her nose. "No fair implying disaster so early in the morning."

She smiled at him, unable to resist his buoyant mood. "Okay. What would you like to hear?"

"Compliments," he said, cupping her bottom with both hands and pulling her close.

She laced her fingers behind his neck and looked up at him. "I like the way you smell."

He chuckled. "Now?"

"Now, but before, too."

"Mmm." He kneaded her soft flesh and his gaze softened. "I know what you mean. There's nothing like the scent of lovemaking with the right person."

"Last night was the most wonderful time in bed I've ever had," she admitted.

"I'm glad."

"But there's more," she said, warming to her subject, "I like to look at you, even in clothes."

He laughed. "And?"

"I like your honesty, your caring, your self-assured manner and even your whistling in the morning."

He slipped both hands along her ribcage to the swell of her breasts. "Thank you for such wonderful compliments," he murmured. "I shouldn't have let you go first. You swiped all my lines."

She swayed slightly as his hands stroking her breasts fired the memory of their loving. She swallowed. "Except that I don't whistle in the morning."

"I'll teach you," he said, gathering her into his arms and brushing her lips. "The first step is to pucker up. Yeah, like that. And then…and then…oh, to hell with whistling," he murmured, capturing her mouth. He kissed her thoroughly before lifting his head. "This is dangerous."

"I know." She nibbled on his bottom lip. "I want to stay here for the rest of the day. I don't want to see Durnberg or play his stupid games."

"Neither do I," he said, pulling back with a sigh and massaging her shoulders, "but it would be pointless for both of us to lose this account. Some day soon we will spend the whole day in bed, after we've settled this business with Ham."

She cocked her head to one side. "Even if I win the account? Will you still want to go to bed with me then?"

"Lady, I can't imagine any conditions that would keep me from wanting to make love to you. I'd have to be in my grave to ignore those long sexy legs and those uptilted breasts."

"Maybe I should get that in writing. Because I really think I have a chance to get Durnberg's business, Max. I'm warning you ahead of time."

He grinned. "Okay. Consider me warned. And you'd better hop in the shower unless you plan to play golf like that. And if you play golf like that, I won't be able to play at all. So have some sympathy, okay?"

"Okay." She kissed him swiftly on the lips and maneuvered around him to the bathroom. "And if you have any time left, would you please try to fix this room? It looks as if someone's had an orgy in here."

"I was looking for the right word to describe last night," Max said. "I guess that's it."

Clare poked her head around the bathroom door. "Max, I want you to know that I don't usually—what's so funny?"

"You," he said, grinning. "You're so worried that I'll think you're a loose woman. Have you ever considered that my behavior could be interpreted that way, too? It works both ways."

She looked at him in surprise. "You're right. The old double standard strikes again. Max, I do believe you're a liberated man."

"I try."

"Thanks for the insight," she said and smiled as she returned to the task of showering. After adjusting the water temperature she stuck her head out of the door again. "Oh, and Max?"

"Yeah?" He had her dress in one hand and her bra in another.

"Although you did go to bed with me on the first date, I still respect you this morning."

His laughter followed her into the shower and she thought to herself that morning had never felt so good. She'd shampooed her hair and sudsed herself all over when Max called into the steamy bathroom.

"Phone's ringing!"

She thrust back the shower curtain. "Don't answer it, for Lord's sake!"

He glanced at her and started to untie the towel around his waist. "I'd rather you didn't, either."

"No, Max, I have to." Stepping out of the tub she grabbed a towel and trailed soapy water across the carpet to the bedside phone. "Hello?"

"Clare, dear! You took so long to answer that I thought you weren't there."

"Mom? What's the problem at this time in the morning?"

"I wanted to catch you before your day started," her mother said. "I hope I didn't wake you."

"No." Clare gazed at Max, still in his towel, leaning in the bathroom doorway with his arms crossed. "I was in the shower."

"I'm sorry," her mother apologized. "Shall I call you back?"

"That's okay. What is it?" Clare shivered and tried to wrap the towel closer while Max retreated to the bathroom, she supposed to finish getting ready.

"One of your clients is angry with me, but I'm doing what you said, and not giving people extras, like last time."

"Which client, Mom?" A warm washcloth glided over Clare's back and she let out a startled exclamation. When she turned, Max was standing behind her with the cloth and the ice bucket full of warm water.

"Clare? Is something wrong?"

"No, Mom. Go ahead." Clare tried to focus on her mother's story as Max removed her towel and began sponging the sticky soap from her body. His ministrations felt so good that she couldn't bear to make him stop.

"Well, Mrs. Bodiddle came in yesterday afternoon," her mother said, "right after I called you, and I hated to bother you again so soon. But then I couldn't sleep for worrying about it."

"Mom," Clare prompted. "Just tell me."

"All right. You remember, dear, that Mrs. Bodiddle is a rather large woman?"

"Yes, Mom, quite large." Clare rolled her eyes at Max, who had finished her back and made her switch the receiver to the other ear while he rinsed her arm. She missed the first part of her mother's next sentence.

". . . and fell on top of her car. Dented in the roof something terrible."

"What? What fell?"

"Mrs. Bodiddle! Honestly, Clare, are you listening?"

"Yes," Clare said, and felt herself beginning to get silly. Max was guiding the washcloth over her breasts and down her ribs, tickling her gently with each swipe, and her mother was telling her that Mrs. Bodiddle, all two hundred plus pounds of her, had fallen on the roof of her car. "How did she do that, exactly?" Clare asked, trying to keep the laughter from her voice.

"Checking the shingles on her roof, if you can imagine! Of all the foolish things for a woman of her size to be doing. So she's checking the shingles and loses her balance and blam! Falls off the roof onto her new Toyota. Naturally I told her there was no coverage for such a thing."

"But Mom, there is," Clare said, giddy and nearly out of control as Max continued to sponge her down. "Falling objects," she added, almost choking on her laughter.

"Really? Oh, dear."

"Just call her back this morning, Mom," Clare managed to say. "If she came in to report this, I guess she's not hurt too seriously herself."

"Not really. A few bruises, but nothing broken according to the X rays she had taken. All that padding, I guess. But Clare, the Toyota is a disaster."

"Tell her she can have it fixed." Clare figured she'd better get off the phone quickly, for lots of reasons. Max was finished with his work and was beginning to play. "Anything else?"

"No. I'm planning a wonderful day with your files."

"That's good," Clare said, swallowing a giggle. "'Bye, Mom."

"Goodbye, dear."

Clare hung up the phone and collapsed against Max with helpless laughter.

"What?" he said, chuckling as he put down the washcloth and bucket of water so he could wrap her in his arms. "Surely my sponge bath wasn't so funny."

"Max," she said, gasping for breath, "you have no idea what it's like, talking to your mother on the telephone about a client who fell on her car while your lover, unknown to that mother, is sponging soap from your body, and it tickles, not to mention giving you . . . other sensations."

"Your client fell on her car?"

"Mrs. Bodiddle, who is, shall we say, on the portly side, fell off her roof onto the car. She wasn't hurt, but the Toyota is in intensive care." Clare grinned. "I shouldn't make fun of the situation, but—"

Max chuckled, which fueled her own amusement, and soon they fell to the bed convulsed with uncontrolled laughter.

"I suppose . . . it's not that funny," Clare said, wiping her eyes and giggling some more.

"Maybe it's the lack of sleep," Max said, a wide smile still on his face.

"We're punchy."

"Yeah, that's it." Max's smile slowly faded. "And what I wouldn't give to make love to you right this minute."

"Oh, Max." She gazed at him as strong emotion gripped her. "It isn't fair," she said, battling her regret. "We shouldn't have to get dressed and run around the golf course with Durnberg right now."

"No, it isn't fair." He stroked her cheek. "But that's what we're going to do. I'm going over to my side and close the connecting door. I'll get dressed and rumple my covers so it will look as if I've slept in my bed."

"I didn't think of that. Max, is there any chance we can keep this a secret?"

"We can try," he said, kissing her softly. "Now hurry," he added, swinging his legs over the edge of the bed. "And the next time I see you, we'll behave like distant friends. Follow my lead."

"I will."

"We'll be fine," he said, gazing at her one last time. Then he was gone.

Clare followed his advice and hurried through the rest of her preparations. She dried her hair and caught it up in a ponytail. Then she dressed quickly in pink shorts, a white sleeveless blouse and her running shoes. Finally she policed the bedroom one last time to remove any evidence of her eventful night. She smoothed the bed as best she could and put the box of condoms back in the bathroom vanity drawer just as her doorbell buzzed.

Within minutes she was seated beside Max in the back seat of the Mercedes with Ham in the front next to Santiago, the chauffeur.

"Did you two have a restful night?" Ham asked, hooking his arm over the front seat and smiling back at them.

"Wonderful," Max said easily. "I can't speak for Clare, of course, but it's amazing how the salt air relaxes me."

Clare was in awe of Max's command of himself. And somehow he'd answered Durnberg without lying. What he'd said was true; they'd been very relaxed once the decision to spend the night together had been made. This morning they'd behaved as if they'd known each other for a long time.

"Well, you both look wonderful," Ham said, scrutinizing Clare.

Bravely she met his stare. "Thank you," she said evenly. If Max could keep his cool, she thought, so could she. "By the way, what will I do for golf shoes this morning? Can I play in these?" She crossed one foot over her knee to display her running shoes.

"You can, if you wish, but I'll be glad to treat you to a pair of—"

"These will be fine," Clare said, eager not to place herself in Ham's debt any more than necessary. "Besides," she added with a smile, "if I don't play well I can blame my shoes." *There*, she thought. *I can make light-hearted comments, just like Max, despite the fact that my hand is lying on the seat inches from his hand, the hand that only an hour ago was caressing—* She pulled her thoughts to an abrupt halt, before she ruined the effect with a blush.

"As you wish," Ham said. "Did either of you order any breakfast from room service this morning?"

"No," Clare said. "At least, I didn't," she added quickly. "Perhaps Max did."

"Didn't get around to it, Ham," Max said. "Stayed in bed too long."

Clare glanced out the window for fear her reaction to Max's last statement would be obvious to Durnberg.

"You?" Ham chided. "The original morning person? I figured you'd be up by six, take a jog down the beach and order a sizable breakfast from room service, the way you always do."

"Must be my age," Max said. "Or your very comfortable beds. You know, Ham, those of us with back trouble appreciate that firm support."

Clare leaned her elbow on the armrest and covered her grin with her hand. Max was deliberately making himself out to be a deteriorating middle-aged man for Ham's benefit, and from the way Ham was shaking his head and looking at Max, the ruse was working.

"Max, I almost hate to drag you out on that tennis court this afternoon. Tennis elbow, heart trouble, bad back. You're a physical wreck, man."

"Ain't it the truth," Max agreed. "Care to spot me a few points?"

"Not yet, on the off-chance that you're sandbagging," Ham said. "Let's find out how your golf game is before I start passing out gifts. But I will order some sandwiches and cold drinks to take along. The least you can do is keep your strength up with food."

"Yeah, I suppose I should keep my strength up," Max said, stretching his little finger across the space on the seat to brush against Clare's. "I'd hate to spoil anyone's fun."

She swallowed hard and prayed that she'd make it through this day. That single, infinitesimal touch from Max had been enough to start her insides churning with desire, and she wouldn't be able to hold him again until the dark night created a cloak to disguise their passion.

Fortunately for her, Max arranged the golf game in a way that helped Clare maintain her composure. He took a cart alone and suggested that she ride with Durnberg. She played passably well, surprising herself. Perhaps, she thought, making love to Max all night long had given her an extra jolt of adrenaline and self-confidence.

Max, however, scored poorly, although when Clare watched him drive off the tee she caught her breath at the supple grace of his body. But he would follow his masterful drives with botched chip shots and missed putts. He joked with Ham that he needed glasses, but Clare didn't believe a single word. Max was deliberately losing in order to further convince Ham that he was over the hill in everything, including his former expertise with women. Knowing that Max was a true competitor, she cherished the sacrifice that he was making in order to protect her.

Because she wasn't riding in the same golf cart with Max, Clare was sheltered from the temptations his nearness might bring, but she also had to spend more time with Durnberg, who used the opportunity to describe in detail all his recent golfing victories.

"You know," he said, turning to her as he braked the cart to a stop near the seventh green, "I thought for certain you and old Max would be billing and cooing by now, but either the guy's lost it, or you've decided to stick to business."

"Business *is* what I'm here for," Clare said.

Durnberg nodded. "Apparently so. Well, I looked over your proposal pretty carefully last night, and I'm impressed. You've put several bells and whistles in that Max hasn't bothered with, and I like bells and whistles."

"I'm glad you approve of the extras," she said, "but my main focus is providing you with a single agent for both resorts and for your health and life insurance needs. In the long run, despite the bells and whistles, your coverage will be simpler."

A trickle of nervous perspiration slid between her breasts. Durnberg sounded as if he might seriously consider her proposal. She might indeed win the account. And what, she wondered, would that do to her newfound relationship with Max?

"One agent for the whole works," Durnberg said, nodding. "It has a certain appeal. But I don't know. I've been with Max for a lot of years. I'm used to having the guy around."

So you can kick him once in a while, Clare thought. But she didn't kid herself that Max would willingly give up this account, kicks or not. The money was too good for anyone to sneer at it. "Do you have any specific questions?" Clare asked, wanting to get away from a discussion of Max.

"A few, but they can wait. Come on. Let's see if old Max three-putts this green, too."

Clare climbed from her seat and walked to the back of the cart to pull her putter from the bag. She had another question to ask, one that needed an answer, yet she hated to hear what the answer was. "Ham, I don't want to rush you on this, but . . . how much longer do you anticipate that Max and I will be staying? My agency in Flagstaff does need attention, and—"

"Staying?" Ham placed his finger under the middle of his putter shaft and balanced the club for several seconds. Clare believed he enjoyed every moment of being in control of two peoples' lives. "I think perhaps you'll be able to go home tomorrow," he said. "I'll make my decision in the morning."

Clare nodded and glanced at Max who was striding toward the green, his putter in one hand. She had one more night with him before Durnberg chose the lucky winner. One more night. After that she had no guarantees, and she knew it.

10

A YELLOW TENNIS BALL popped like gunfire against taut racket strings as Max and Durnberg flailed away on center court. Clare's neck ached from swiveling her head as the men drove the ball back and forth across the green net. Finally she decided to concentrate on Max.

From the shade of a canopied seating area, cold lemonade on a small table at her side, she watched the sweat soak through his white cotton shirt and darken the area between his shoulder blades and across his lean stomach. He was holding his own in the match, despite having almost no sleep in the past thirty-six hours. She hoped that he wasn't playing with such ferocity because of her presence. He had nothing to prove to her, and the first chance she had, she'd tell him so.

She suspected, however, that this pounding, sweat-soaked effort helped release his tensions concerning Durnberg far better than a gentlemanly game of golf. She caught the grin of satisfaction when he forced Ham to dive for a particularly well-placed shot.

He won the serve and moved to the back of the court where he snagged one-handed the two balls that Durnberg lobbed in succession across the net toward him. After placing his right foot at the serving line, he bounced the first ball hard against the professional-quality surface, green and smooth as a pool table.

As he crouched, gathering the force to launch the ball across the net, Clare squirmed in her seat, restless with pent-up desire. He gave her a piercing glance, as if guessing her thoughts. Then he tossed the ball in the air and brought his arm over in a blinding arc that smashed the ball into the opposite court.

Durnberg missed the serve. Clare opened her mouth to cheer and fortunately closed it again before she'd landed herself in trouble. Instead she managed a luke-warm "nice shot" and took a drink of her lemonade.

So far, by using great restraint, she'd favored neither player with her praise. She hoped that Max's skill had kept Durnberg busy enough that he hadn't had a chance to observe her facial expressions, which were more dif-ficult to control.

As Max prepared for his next serve, a young man with a nametag designating him as a resort employee approached Clare. She glanced at the portable tele-phone he was carrying and winced. Her mother again, she'd bet.

After learning from the young man that the call was indeed for her, Clare picked up the receiver with a si-lent prayer that her mother hadn't fouled up anything else. Maybe Mrs. Bodiddle had called the insurance commission about her dented roof before Clare's mother could rectify the mistake about coverage.

"Clare, dear, how is it going?" her mother chirped.

"Very well, Mom. Durnberg seems to like my pro-posal. Why are you calling?" Clare tried not to think about the long-distance charges her mother was accu-mulating. If Durnberg took the coverage, it wouldn't really matter.

"I'm just so proud of myself, Clare, that I had to call you. The files are done, and now when you open a drawer you see a rainbow!"

"That's neat, Mom," Clare said, smiling in relief. "And what about Mrs. Bodiddle?"

"She was a little frosty at first, but I apologized profusely and didn't once mention how stupid I thought that accident was."

"Good, good."

"And Clare, I know you think my baked goodies are a waste of time, but when I offered Mrs. Bodiddle a home-baked coffee cake to make up for my mistake, she sounded quite delighted."

Clare laughed. "In this case, I imagine it was exactly the right compensation." She watched Max rush the net and slam the ball out of Durnberg's reach.

"I thought so," Clare's mother said, sounding pleased with herself. "And wait until you see these files. They'll knock your eyes out."

Clare's smile faded as she remembered something. "Mom, where are the old folders now?"

"Those ugly things? In the dumpster, thank goodness."

"Mom, did you copy the notes I had written inside the folders before you threw them away?"

"That scribbled stuff? I couldn't read it, Clare. Some of it looked like doodles, and I—"

"Then you didn't copy it."

"No . . . was I supposed to? I didn't think—"

Clare turned away from the tennis match and spoke urgently into the phone. "You've got to get those folders back right away."

"Get them back?"

"Yes," Clare said, trying not to panic. "I know the information was garbled, but I understood it, and some of those notes aren't duplicated anywhere else. I have to have those folders." She thought quickly. "Today's

Wednesday, and the garbage pickup isn't until first thing in the morning. Joel can help you get them out."

"Um, all right, dear. I'll take care of it." Her mother sounded completely deflated.

"Thanks, Mom. And I appreciate all of your work, really. But I do need those folders."

"All right. I'll get them."

"Oh, and Mom, I'll be home sometime tomorrow. Durnberg is making his decision in the morning."

"He is?" Some of her mother's enthusiasm returned. "Well, I just know he'll choose your coverage."

"Keep your fingers crossed."

"I will, dear. Goodbye for now, and good luck."

"Thanks, Mom. You're a peach." Clare hung up the phone and returned it to the young man who had hovered a discreet distance away. "Thank you," she said, and reached for her wallet to give him a tip.

"Oh, no ma'am," he said, backing away as he saw her intent. "Mr. Durnberg told us not to accept any tips from you or Mr. Armstrong. Mr. Durnberg's taken care of all that."

"Oh." Clare glanced back at the court and noticed that Max and Durnberg had left their rackets leaning against the net and were walking toward her, apparently to take a break. Durnberg hailed the young man before he got away and placed an order for three more lemonades.

"What's the score?" Clare asked Max as he sat in a chair on the other side of her small table.

"If you stayed off the telephone once in a while you wouldn't have to ask," Max said with a teasing smile.

"My mother again," she replied.

"Your mother?" Durnberg said, joining them and sitting next to Max. "No problems at home, I trust?"

"No, she just—" Clare glanced at Max and saw the glint of humor in his eyes. She guessed that he was remembering this morning, and the story about the woman who'd fallen on her car. Maybe he was also remembering what he'd been doing during that call. Clare looked away quickly. "My mother likes to keep in touch," she said. "But with the distraction I lost track of the score. What is it?"

"Somehow, Max has tied it up, three-three," Durnberg said. "Dumb luck, I guess."

"That's how I'd explain it," Max said as their lemonade arrived and they both reached for their glasses.

Clare watched them gulp the cold drink and hoped they weren't killing themselves. "You're putting on quite a show," she said, aiming her comment at both of them but intending it for Max. "I hope you're not overdoing it, just to impress the gallery."

Max polished off his lemonade and grinned at her. "Is the gallery impressed?"

"Not if both of you collapse when it's over," she said, guarding her response by leaning forward to glance over at Durnberg.

"I've never felt better," Durnberg boasted, although he was breathing hard and his shirt was plastered to his chest. "I don't know about the old man over there," he added, jerking a thumb at Max. "This lemonade is for his benefit, you know. Used to be we'd drink beer during a match."

"I'm glad you're not drinking it now," Clare said. "November never felt this hot in Flagstaff, I can tell you that."

"And not a single breeze today," Durnberg added, wiping his face with a towel. "Which doesn't bode well for the windsurfing later this afternoon. Maybe we'll have to change the plan and water ski, instead. Do you water ski, Clare?"

"Not well," Clare said, thinking that as tired as she felt, she'd probably drown if she had to attempt such a strenuous activity. She couldn't imagine how Max would survive, either, even if he could water ski. She'd been able to rest a little during the tennis match, but Max had worn himself out even more.

"Then we'll teach you to ski, Max and I, won't we, old buddy?"

"Sure," Max said without flinching.

Yet Clare noticed the heavy weariness around his eyes. Despite the energy he'd displayed on the tennis court, he was exhausted. "Ham," she said, searching for a way to free Max for a much-needed nap, "maybe instead of doing either of those things, you and I should sit down and go over the questions you have about my proposal." She didn't realize that her suggestion might sound like aggressive business tactics until she saw the look on Max's face. "I mean…um…perhaps Max also has some things he'd like to discuss with you, and if we're leaving tomorrow—"

"Tomorrow?" Max stared at Durnberg. "You didn't mention that to me, Ham."

"Hadn't quite gotten to it, old buddy. Clare asked me about it on the golf course and I told her that I'd make my decision between your coverage and hers in the morning."

"I see." Max's gaze flicked between them. "In that case, maybe I'd better ask if you have any questions you'd like to ask me, Ham, now that you've studied Clare's proposal."

"Perhaps I do have one," Durnberg said, hanging the towel around his neck. "How long would it take you to get licensed in Florida?"

Max paused. "I don't know. A few weeks, maybe. I'd have to establish a contact here, of course. I didn't think that was important to you, Ham. You have an excellent agent here, and me in Flagstaff. Why take a chance on one agent spreading himself—" He stopped to glance at Clare. "Or I should say *herself*, thin by taking care of two very large accounts?"

Durnberg smirked, and Clare felt sick to her stomach. He loved every minute of this, while she wished for a magic wand to whisk her away from this painful scene.

"I understand," Durnberg said, "that computers help tremendously when you're talking about volume of business. Have you bought one yet, Max?"

"No, I haven't," Max said quietly.

Clare couldn't look at him. For the first time he was entertaining the idea that Clare might take the account away and she couldn't bear to see the effect that might have on him. He'd said that none of this was personal, that they'd continue their relationship regardless of who won. Clare's stomach churned as she wondered if he'd really meant it.

"Well!" Durnberg stood abruptly and regarded both of them with satisfaction. "This isn't the place to discuss all that, is it? Anyway, you've answered my questions for now, Max. Let's finish our match and grab a bite to eat. Then perhaps Clare and I should sit down with her charts for a while."

Max nodded. "All right," he said evenly, rising from his chair, as well. "While you're talking with Clare maybe I'll stretch out on that comfortable bed in my room and take a little siesta."

Clare felt a pang of regret, as she was certain Max had intended her to. She could guess what he might be thinking, that she'd turned everything, including the ride in the golf cart with Durnberg this morning, to her advantage. But hadn't she warned him that she would?

"Say, Max," Durnberg said, giving him a sly wink, "I have an idea where we might have our business discussion this evening." He glanced at Clare. "Remember the way we capped off your visit a year ago?"

"Forget it, Ham," Max said abruptly. "Not this time."

"Such a shame." Durnberg sighed. "Nothing's like the old days, is it Max?"

"What are you two talking about?" Clare asked.

"Oh, Max and I took in a couple of 'shows' last year," Durnberg said, putting enough emphasis on the word that Clare guessed they were strip shows.

"Oh."

Max's expression clouded with anger. "Ham, let's not discuss—"

"I don't know why not," Durnberg interrupted. "You have nothing to hide. I never did convince you to take one of those girls home. I just thought you needed consolation after the divorce. Maybe you still do," he added, glancing at Clare. "Max used to be a fun insurance agent to have around, but not anymore. I don't know why."

Clare figured any move of Durnberg's was premeditated. At the moment he might be fishing around, trying to discover Max's feelings toward Clare. To make matters worse, he might guess the truth, that Max was declining the invitation to carouse with Durnberg because of her. Max was falling on his sword, and she didn't want victory that way. "I think you both should go," she said. "I'll have a quiet meal in my room and rest."

"Clare," Max said, frowning, "that's nonsense. We can all have dinner here together."

Clare laughed and glanced away. "My goodness, what does a lady have to say to convince you that she wants to be alone for the evening?"

"Hey, Max," Durnberg said. "I think you just got dumped. Better come with me tonight."

"Okay," Max said, staring at Clare with a puzzled expression. "I will. Come on, Ham," he added, standing. "Let's finish this match. I've toyed with you long enough. Now it's time to put you away for good."

"So you still think you can take me, do you?" Durnberg threw down the towel. "We'll see about that."

With a sense of frustration, Clare watched them walk away. She was probably a fool to send him away tonight to watch scantily clad women and solidify his position with Durnberg. Yet she sensed the tide was turning in her favor and Max shouldn't be deprived of the strengths he'd always had with Durnberg.

Funny that when she'd dreamed of taking the account away from Max, she'd imagined the thrill of pulling off such a coup. Instead she felt completely confused, afraid that she'd be miserable whether she won or lost the account because her emotions were hopelessly involved in the outcome. Somehow she had to regain the belief that Max's creed was true—business was only business.

As the tennis match continued, Max surprised Clare by trouncing Durnberg the next two games and making good his boast. She'd always thought he could do it, but she'd also thought that he might let Durnberg win.

Durnberg came off the court grumbling. "I think something's wrong with this damned racket," he said as they neared the canopy where Clare sat. "The strings are too loose. How can I expect to play my best game with faulty equipment?"

"Looks fine to me," Max answered, unperturbed. "I think you need more practice, old buddy."

"I can take you, Max, I know it. Let me get another racquet and we'll play again."

"No dice," Max said, smiling. "If you want a rematch you'll have to make it another day. I'm done in, and you wouldn't want to take advantage of a tired old man, would you?"

"In the morning, then, before you leave."

"We'll see."

Clare was amazed at Max's independent attitude, but slowly she began to understand his strategy. By beating Durnberg, Max was giving him a reason to keep Max's coverage. Unless Durnberg stayed with Max, he wouldn't have another chance to prove he was better than his old rival at tennis.

"Anyone for a swim before lunch?" Durnberg asked as they left the courts with Clare in the middle between the two men. "I seldom swim in the ocean but the pool would feel nice."

"Not for me, thanks," Max said. "In fact, if you don't mind I'll have lunch in my room. I wasn't kidding about that nap. You've worn me out, old buddy."

"Max, you do surprise me," Durnberg said, shaking his head. "But I don't want you dragging around on me tonight, so run along. How about you, Clare? A swim and some lunch by the pool?"

"I'm not very hungry," she replied, not wanting to spend any more time than necessary alone with Durnberg. "Why don't I take a shower and meet you in your office in an hour?"

Durnberg clucked his tongue like a disapproving school teacher. "I obviously have a couple of wimps on my hands. All right, then. I'll see you in my office in an hour, Clare. Or would you rather take a nap first, too?"

Would she ever. Clare fantasized for a short moment about escaping to the privacy of the room with Max. Yet Max might not welcome her there, now that he understood that she was a serious competitor for the account. "I'll be in your office in an hour," she said. "I don't need a nap."

Beside her, under his breath so that only she could hear, Max muttered one quick statement. "Or anything else, apparently."

Clare questioned him with a glance but he looked straight ahead as if he hadn't spoken. She waited until Durnberg had left for the pool and they were walking alone back to the cottages before she pursued the matter. "Max, I couldn't have you turning down his invitation because of me," she said as they followed the narrow asphalt path to their duplex.

"Why not? You appear to be on the fast track."

"You need to go with him tonight."

"Probably. But for one thing I've lost my appetite for that sort of thing, and for another I had the crazy idea that you might want to spend some time with me." He lifted his racket and swatted at a branch that protruded onto the path.

"I do, but Max, there's a very good chance I'll get this account." Above them, a sea gull cried, and Clare glanced up to watch it soar toward the turquoise waters of the Gulf. If only she and Max could be that free.

"I'm beginning to realize that."

"So protect yourself, damn it! Don't stay home with me tonight and give him another reason to drop you."

Max chuckled with relief. "And I was afraid I'd lost my charm."

"Hardly."

He glanced at her. "So what are you doing, giving me advice about how to save the account with Durnberg?"

She took a deep breath. "Maybe."

"Doesn't make sense, Clare."

She returned his glance. "It didn't make sense for you to give me advice earlier, either, but you did. I'm repaying you."

"Thanks a lot." They'd reached her door, and he turned to her. "Now I have to go out and watch gyrating bodies that I could care less about, when I'd rather be—"

"What?" she murmured, smiling.

"Making love to someone I care a great deal about," he said in a low voice.

"Maybe you can have both."

"You'll wait up for me?"

"Absolutely not. I'll be in bed when you get home."

"That has an inviting sound to it," he said, rubbing the metal edge of the racket gently along her forearm. "What's your favorite way to wake up?"

Passion stretched and opened within her at his touch. "I'll let you experiment," she said, gazing into his eyes and remembering how well he'd loved her.

He sighed. "How much time before you have to meet him at his office?"

"Not enough."

"Probably not, especially for what I have in mind."

"Max, you need rest. Go to sleep."

"Damn, but I hate to waste time that way."

"I know, but afternoons are risky for being together, anyway. Tonight, after you've gotten rid of Durnberg, is the best time."

"You can say that again."

She took a long, quivering breath. "Yeah."

"Now get into your own room, before I change my mind about all of this and ravish you before your meeting with Durnberg."

So powerful was the pull of her attraction to him that she couldn't move.

"Go," he whispered, and turned her toward the door.

"Max, I—" She looked over her shoulder, but he was already walking away. She could, of course, simply go into her cottage and through the connecting doors to his. If she nestled into his arms, he wouldn't push her away.

Then she remembered how tired he'd looked before the last two games of the tennis match. He'd just finished five grueling games in the hot Florida sun while she'd done nothing more strenuous than talk with her mother on the telephone.

Clare thought of the reason behind Max's decision to take a nap. He wanted to rest now so that later he could make glorious love when he returned from his night out with Durnberg. Smiling, Clare entered her cottage and walked directly to her bathroom for a shower. She would let Max sleep.

11

DURNBERG'S QUESTIONS about Clare's proposal were minor ones. They primarily concerned the health and life insurance coverages that she'd added in order to complete the picture of a comprehensive program. He asked for Ron's number and called him while Clare was still there. Even from hearing only one side of the conversation, Clare could tell that Durnberg and Ron liked each other. Perversely she decided that such mutual goodwill reflected poorly on Ron.

After he hung up the phone Durnberg smiled at her, much as a shark could be described as smiling, she thought. Then he leaned back in his swivel chair and looked at her. "I'm impressed with your thoroughness, Clare."

"Thank you."

"Max might have been that thorough once, but after all that business with the surfer and his wife, Max has let a few things go. I don't think he really wanted to pursue the angle of a Florida license so that he could offer coverage on Sugar Sands. Too much trouble with the complications he already has in his life."

Clare couldn't stop herself. "Surfer?" she blurted.

"Didn't I mention that before?"

"No."

"An oversight on my part." Durnberg rocked back in his chair. "You see, our Max has always been a hard worker, but he let his relationship with Adele slip away from him in the process. She'd warned him about being a workaholic, but I guess he didn't take her seriously." Durnberg seemed to relish every sad detail of the marriage's disintegration. Clare wondered if Ham had once desired Adele himself.

"So," Durnberg continued, "when the surfer from San Diego blew into town to open a branch of his clothing store, Adele took the boys down, to outfit them for school, you know. This happy-go-lucky guy who could make money and have fun at the same time charmed her away from Max. The poor guy hasn't been nearly as effective an agent since then."

Clare's heart ached. And now she was taking business away from Max when he was down. But what could she do? Retract her proposal? That would be unfair to Joel and her mother, not to mention her own career. She could commit business suicide by behaving so unprofessionally, especially if Durnberg spread the word about what she'd done.

Now she also understood Max's reaction to Durnberg's teasing remarks about surfers. The subject was a sore one, for good reason. Sadly Clare compared her original image of Max with her new one. Instead of the arrogant, money-hungry businessman she'd thought him to be before they'd met, he now appeared more like a wounded bear.

"Well, Clare, I think that takes care of our business," Ham said, standing. He held out his hand. "Thank you for explaining everything, and I'll give you my decision over breakfast. Shall we say about nine in the morning?"

"That's fine." She winced at his handshake, which squeezed her fingers together painfully. *Sadistic bully,* she thought. Yet she couldn't be expected to like all her clients, she reasoned, flexing her tingling hand after he released it. Hadn't Max said that personalities have nothing to do with business?

"I can arrange for your flight home about noon, if that's convenient."

"Perfectly convenient."

"You know, I thought for sure you and Max would be romantically entangled by now."

From somewhere she found the courage to look him in the eye. "That wouldn't be very businesslike, would it?"

Durnberg shook his head and gave her a grudging smile. "You're tough, Clare Pemberton, tougher than I thought you'd be. I still think Max is attracted to you. You noticed that he wanted to stay here tonight."

"He was being polite."

"No, he was being hopeful, but you squashed that right quick. I almost expected you to say that you had to wash your hair. Doesn't he interest you at all? Max is usually such a lady-killer."

"Max is a very nice man," Clare said, hating herself for sounding so prim, "but my first objective in coming here was to get your business, Ham."

"Well, you just might. I'll see you in the morning."

"Fine. And Ham, thank you for everything," she made herself say. "You've been very kind with your hospitality." *With ulterior motives at every turn*, she added silently. Durnberg had used all available opportunities to manipulate her and Max.

"I've enjoyed having you both as visitors to Sugar Sands," Durnberg said. "Perhaps the three of us can do this again sometime."

"Perhaps." Clare couldn't imagine under what circumstances. If she won the account, she might be forced to return here occasionally, but surely Max wouldn't be part of that picture. Even if he accepted his loss with equanimity, she could only expect so much tolerance from him. "Have a nice evening," she said over her shoulder as she left the office.

Durnberg laughed. "One thing about the guy—he knows how to have fun. I expect another memorable night with Max Armstrong."

That makes two of us, Clare thought, her mind busy with what she'd learned about Max, and what she had yet to discover.

MAX NOTICED that the brunette on the small stage was looking directly at him. Smiling, she shimmied her unfettered breasts in his direction. He realized that he must have been staring at her. She had no way of knowing that it was a vacant stare, while his thoughts were occupied with another woman, a long-legged blonde home in bed, waiting for him.

The parade of scantily clothed women he'd endured tonight had acted somewhat like remote-control foreplay. None of the dancers looked like Clare, but often the curve of a breast or a creamy length of thigh would remind him of the night before with Clare. Instantly he was aroused as his memory filled in her moans of delight and the dewy sheen of her skin as he'd loved her.

Seated across the small round table from him, Durnberg shouted and waved a twenty in the air. The brunette shimmied faster and began a sinuous descent from the stage into the audience amid clapping and cheers.

"Hey, we got one, Max," Ham crowed in delight, banging the table with the flat of his hand. "Between your good-looking mug and my money we're a great team. Look at those knockers. Woo!"

"Oh, God." Max could tell she was focusing on him most of the time, with occasional glances at Ham's money waving in the air. Stoically Max met the come-hither glance of the woman. He had to play the game to some extent. Ham had already accused him of being dull and boring when he'd refused the advances of dancers at the first place they'd stopped. Finally Max had suggested they move on and had vowed to himself on the way that he'd put up a good front at the second place and get the whole thing over as soon as possible.

Unfortunately he'd set a bad precedent last year. The divorce papers had arrived the day before he'd left for Florida with Ham, and he'd been in the mood to drink a little too much and flirt with anything in sight to salve his battered ego.

Ham had enjoyed himself immensely that night, Max remembered, because Max's enthusiasm brought most of the dancers to their table at one time or another, and Ham had ended up spending the rest of the night with one. Max hadn't, realizing halfway into a proposition he was making that he had absolutely no desire to have sex with this stranger.

Ham seemed to prefer strangers, Max noticed. His fear of intimacy had kept him a bachelor who was nearly devoid of friends of either gender. Ham pretended that Max was a friend, and that was the weapon in Max's arsenal when the decision had to be made about which insurance coverage to take.

The brunette was wending her way toward them. She stopped at a few tables along the way but kept her attention mostly on Max. She was a good dancer, he had to give her that. For a moment he enjoyed a brief fantasy of how Clare would look, dancing seductively like that, privately, for him. Lord, how he wanted her!

The woman's hair was done in a style similar to Clare's, a smooth curve falling almost to her shoulders. That might have been why he'd thought of Clare in her place, Max thought. Other than the hairstyle, nothing reminded him of Clare.

Her legs were shapely but lacked the long grace of Clare's. The dancer wore black fishnet stockings attached to a red satin garter belt. Garter belts. Max sucked in his breath as he remembered how Clare had peeled off her stockings one at a time on the beach. He'd kept his cool pretty well until then.

Not that a garter belt could make much difference if he didn't want a woman in the first place. And he didn't want this one. Her breasts were large, probably helped along by silicone, he thought, and each one was tipped with a red satin flower shaped like a daisy.

Every visible inch of her was golden brown, either from the Florida sun, or more likely from a lamp, Max surmised. He'd never been much for all-over tans, and the pale swimsuit outlined on Clare's body when he'd undressed her last night had driven him crazy.

As the pulsing music continued the woman danced closer and leaned toward him to allow the satin daisies to brush his cheeks. The crowd shouted its approval. Her scent, heavy and floral, assailed him.

He didn't want her, but she was a woman, and her nearness brought vivid memories of Clare—Clare beneath him, her body undulating with the rhythm of their passion. He fought the surge of desire, not wanting to acknowledge a reaction that belonged to Clare and not to this unknown dancer.

The music stopped and the woman slithered onto his lap. "How're you doing, honey?" she crooned, looping one arm around his neck and settling herself against his chest. The music started again and another dancer appeared on stage.

"Fine," he said gruffly.

"Aw, Max, if you're gonna act like that, let her come over here," Ham complained. "Hey, sweetheart, I may not be as pretty as he is, but I'm a lot more friendly."

The woman glanced at Max and ran a dark red fingernail along his jawline. "Maybe he's the strong, silent type. I like that in a man."

"Naw, he's just grouchy," Ham said. "Besides, I'm also richer than he is."

The dancer gazed into Max's eyes and smiled her understanding of his reluctance. "I'm not prejudiced against rich men," she said to Ham, gliding from Max's lap and making her way around the table to Ham's. "Besides, when I was coming over here, I couldn't make up my mind which of you two handsome studs I like best. Your friend was closer, that's all."

"Yeah, sure," Ham said, his words slurring a little from the drinks he'd had. "Women always like Max better. I'm used to it."

"But I don't, honey," the woman insisted, rubbing her breasts against his chest.

"In that case, can I buy you a little drink?"

Max relaxed. This might turn out okay, provided the woman accepted the drink. He wished that she hadn't reacted to Ham's offer of money so quickly, but then he wished that women didn't have to do this sort of work at all. With men like Ham around, though, they'd probably continue their trade for a long time.

"Sure you can, if you'll wait until I finish dancing," the woman said. "I have one more number, and I'm through for the evening."

"I can wait," Ham said, looking glassy-eyed as she continued to press herself against him.

"Good. Now stay right here, and I'll be back before you know it."

When she'd left Ham chuckled. "How about that, old buddy? What's the matter, wasn't she your type?"

"Not really."

"How about that one?" Ham pointed to the dancer currently on the stage.

Max knew that he had to get out of there. Needing to hold Clare was becoming an obsession that wracked his body and heated his brain. "You know, Ham, you're not going to believe this, but all that sun today seems to have given me a headache."

"A headache? Come on, Max."

"What can I say, Ham? Your pace must be too much for me."

"Too bad I can't get you on the tennis court right now."

"Yeah, too bad."

"Listen, Max, don't leave. Have another drink. That'll cure your headache, and then we'll find you some nice little lady. I know your problem, buddy. Our friend Clare's got you hot and bothered and she won't put out. We can fix that. One's as good as another," Ham said with a silly grin.

"I don't think another drink will do it, Ham. I need to go to bed," Max said, amused at the truth of his own statement. "Listen, I don't want to rain on your parade, and it sure as heck looks like you have one going, complete with brass band."

"Could be." Ham looked satisfied with himself.

"Then why don't I ask Santiago to drive me home? He can be back before you finish your drink with your friend, and he'll be available to take you . . . wherever you want to go."

"Max, you're not the man you used to be."

"No, Ham, but you still are." Max stood. "Good luck, buddy."

"Thanks. Oh, and Max, we never found time to discuss business tonight. How about meeting at eight in the morning?"

Max glanced at him, knowing full well how much depended on that meeting. "Sure," he said, deliberately nonchalant. "Isn't eight a bit early, considering the friendship you've just formed?"

"You ought to know me better than that, Max." Suddenly he didn't seem quite as drunk as Max had thought he was. "I never let pleasure interfere with business."

"All right," Max said. "Eight it is."

Durnberg picked up his drink. "Sleep tight, old man."

"Thanks." Max had to deliberately slow his steps as he left the bar. Then he walked quickly toward the Mercedes where Santiago sat waiting behind the wheel, listening to music from a portable headset. Max rapped on the window and Santiago looked up, surprised.

"I'm ready to leave," he said, when Santiago rolled down the window.

"What about the boss?"

"You're supposed to come back for him after you drop me off. He might have a lady with him."

Santiago rolled his eyes. "Sometimes I hate this job."

"I know." Max walked around the car and got into the front seat next to Santiago after the driver had unlocked the doors. "So get another job."

"That's the trouble. The money's good, and the family has to eat. You can't thumb your nose at money when you've got responsibilities."

Max sighed. "Don't I know it. One of these days, though, he's going to push me too far. God, how I'd love to tell him what he could do with his precious money."

"I'd sure like to be there if and when it happens."

"The way I feel right now, it may be soon. Move this crate, Santiago, and if you don't mind, I'm putting down the windows. I need some fresh air."

"I can understand."

Max leaned his head back on the seat and took deep breaths of the salt air. How he'd relish telling Durnberg to go to hell, he thought as Santiago whisked him through Sarasota and across the bridge to Longboat Key. But with Adele's demands, and the way business was going recently, he didn't dare.

Besides, even if Adele weren't taking him for everything she could get, he knew that he'd still want to continue doing things for his boys. Teenagers didn't seem to need anything that didn't cost at least a hundred bucks, and being poor wouldn't help him much in that respect.

No, he couldn't afford to have Clare take this account away from him. Besides, he also hated for her to get mixed up with a guy like Durnberg. He'd been handling Durnberg for years, but she had no idea what a slime ball the resort owner could be.

At any rate he could forget all of that for a few hours and concentrate on loving Clare. The ache for her, building all evening, grew sharp and demanding as they drew closer to Sugar Sands. By the time they pulled up at the door of his cottage, he was trembling with desires he'd repressed all day and been reminded of all night.

The doors between his cottage and Clare's were open when he walked in, and soft light glowed from her side. Max felt his groin tighten with a sweet pressure as the urge to touch her again sang through his body.

Shedding clothes as he went, he walked toward her bedroom. From the silence he knew that she was in bed and he wondered whether she'd chosen to wear a nightgown or nothing at all. It didn't matter. He loved equally the teasing excitement of removing a silken garment to reveal her beauty gradually or the fierce and instant joy of gathering her naked into his arms.

The bedside lamp was on low and she was asleep in its gentle light. Also caught in the light's glow was the box she'd brought out of hiding and placed conveniently nearby for their use tonight. He smiled. Another woman might not have left them so obviously in sight, but Clare's forthright manner was one of her most endearing characteristics.

It seemed, he thought with a thrill of anticipation, that he'd be removing a nightgown, a pale blue one of material so sheer that he could see the dusky outline of one nipple as she lay on her side, facing him. A close-fitting midriff of stretch lace circled her small waist.

She'd pushed the white sheet aside as she slept, and it lay crumpled around her hips like a ripple of surf against the blue of her gown. One pink-tipped toe peeked out of the covers near the foot of the bed and he stifled the urge to lean down and kiss it. He wasn't quite ready for her to wake up.

He cast aside the last of his clothes and stood for a moment gazing into her face, so relaxed and open. Her complexion was enhanced by the natural blush of sleep, and her lashes rested in pale semicircles against her cheekbones. He treasured the knowledge that she awaited him without pretense.

Kneeling beside the bed, he breathed in her light fragrance, a far subtler cousin to the dancer's perfume. Her lips, pale pink, were parted, and the sweetness of her breath made him close his eyes as a shudder of desire passed through him.

All the hours of suggestive movements and bare female flesh had left him craving her with an intensity that seemed out of place in this quiet bower. Holding himself in check he brushed her cheek with his lips and kissed the soft lobe of her ear.

"I love you, Clare Pemberton," he whispered, and it seemed as if a tumbler slipped into place and his heart swung open with those words. He knew there was little chance she'd heard him. Better that he not speak that phrase aloud again until after tomorrow's decision, until they knew what Durnberg had in mind.

She stirred and her lashes quivered against her cheeks.

"Wake up, you gorgeous woman," he murmured, louder this time. "I lust for your body."

"Mmm." She rolled to her back and opened her eyes. "Max?" she said sleepily, turning her head to look at him.

"Yes, Max," he said, pulling back the sheet and sliding in beside her. He propped his hand beside her head and leaned over her to gaze into her soft, welcoming eyes. "And Max wants you like you wouldn't believe."

Her dimpled smile winked at him and she circled his neck with both arms. "Max," she said, sighing with sleepy contentment. "You got away from him."

"I had to. I couldn't stand it much longer."

"Stand what?" She sniffed. "You smell of cigarettes and cheap perfume."

"Don't I know it." He buried his face against her neck.

"Whose perfume?"

He caressed her silk-covered hip as he nuzzled her throat. "A dancer's."

"You danced with someone?"

"No." He gathered her nightgown until he reached the hem and could slide his hand beneath it to the warmth of her thigh. "Lord, Clare, but I want you. You're so—"

"Max." She closed her thighs, trapping his hand before it reached its destination. "Why do you have a dancer's perfume on you?"

"Because she sat in my lap." He kissed the swell of her breast. "Please, Clare. It doesn't matter. Just—"

"Just nothing!" She squirmed away from him. "Why was she in your lap?"

He groaned. "She thought I was staring at her, but I wasn't. I was really staring off into space, thinking about you, except that she happened to be occupying the space I was staring into."

"Sure, Max." Her green eyes snapped with indignation. "And what did you do after you enticed her into your lap?"

"Nothing! And I didn't entice her. She got the wrong impression. Then Ham talked her into coming over to sit in his lap, and I beat it out of there to come back to you."

Clare scrambled to a sitting position on the bed. "What was she wearing, this dancer?"

"Red."

"Red what?"

"A garter belt and little satin daisies on her— Damn it, Clare, what difference does it make?"

Clare narrowed her eyes and her words came out like shots from a gun. "Little . . . satin . . . daisies . . . on . . . her . . . *what*?"

"Are you jealous?" He started to grin.

"No!"

"After all, you're the one who insisted I go out with Ham."

"I didn't expect you to fondle women with little satin daisies on their . . . on their . . ."

"Nipples?" he offered helpfully.

"Oh, Max!" She crossed her arms and turned her head away. "How little?" she asked, still not looking at him.

"How little what?"

"Were the daisies?"

"Tiny."

She glared at him. "Max, you're terrible!"

"Hey." He reached for her arm to pull her down but she struggled against him. "Now stop this." He grabbed her other arm and this time succeeded in hauling her down next to him, although she tried to wriggle away.

"How dare you come in here, with her perfume still on you," Clare said, breathing hard from the effort of working to get free. "Some nerve, Max Armstrong."

"Because I couldn't wait," he said, pinning her squirming form beneath his bare chest. "Because I spent the whole blasted evening watching half-naked women and none of them held a candle to you, but they sure reminded me of what I was missing, of who was waiting in this big bed for me."

"But you let her sit in your lap!"

"If I'd pushed her away, I would have embarrassed both of us. Instead I let nature take its course and Ham latched onto her. Once he had a woman for the evening—be still, Clare!—then I was free to come back—" he pressed down against the yielding softness of her breasts "—for this."

"Nothing doing, Max. I—"

His lips descended swiftly on hers and he held her chin when she tried to twist away. He'd give her the benefit of one kiss to change her mind. If she still didn't want him, then maybe he'd been wrong about her, about them.

If he hadn't been so filled with frustrated desire he might have laughed at the way she tried not to kiss him back. But he didn't have time to laugh. He was too busy molding his mouth to hers and challenging the determined barrier of her lips.

Slowly, ever so slowly, her lips softened until finally, with a whimper, she parted them and surrendered the moist inner chamber to his questing tongue. He wooed her mercilessly, deepening the kiss until tenseness slid from her body, melting like the outer shell of an ice cream bar.

Beneath the shell she was pliable and willing—Clare as he'd come home to love her. "Silly woman," he whispered softly when he came up for air. "Don't you know how I feel about you?"

"I thought I did," she said, arching against him, "but that perfume, and the thought of some dancer with almost nothing on."

"Hush," he said, sipping at her lips once more. "Hush and let me love you." Her sigh told him she would do just that, and pent-up emotions flooded through him. Grasping one thin strap in each hand he pulled the top of her nightgown past her breasts and found them pouting and ready for his mouth. Their pale round beauty, tipped with pink the color of raspberry sherbet, excited him far more than the opulent breast he'd viewed all night long.

He rolled her nipple against the roof of his mouth with his tongue and savored her moan of delight. Then he took her more fully into his mouth and exerted a gentle suction that made her toss her head and bury her fingers in his hair. She tasted the way she smelled, like flowers in the sun, or warm bread fresh from the oven. He couldn't get enough of her.

As he sampled her other breast he worked the nightgown lower until it rode on her restless hips. Loving her reminded him of a day at the carnival as a child, when no sooner was one delight relinquished than another presented itself to be enjoyed. Releasing the satisfying fullness of her breast he raised up on one elbow to contemplate the wonder of her bared torso. "I love this view," he murmured, caressing her belly with the flat of his hand. "You look like a mermaid."

"Do you wish I were one," she asked softly, "to satisfy your fantasy?"

"No." He leaned down and flicked his tongue into the indentation of her navel. "Mermaids can't make love," he said, pulling the nightgown lower and kissing a trail as he went. "They don't have the right—" he paused and gently parted her thighs "—equipment."

"Oh, Max," Clare whispered as his tongue found her bud of desire. "Max, you . . . oh . . ."

He received her murmured cries joyfully. The trembling of her legs, the arch of her back, told him how he was affecting her and he loved it. Her passion was building fast, and he could easily give her release now, but he knew the sensation would be sweeter if he held back, and let her climb to the peak again. Slowly he kissed his way back to her breasts, her throat, her chin, her lips.

"I want you," she murmured, kissing him hungrily and pressing the length of her body to his. "I want you so much I can't stand it."

"Don't lose that thought," he said against her mouth. "I'll be right back." He disentangled himself, hating the interruption, and fumbled with the box on the bedside table. As he returned and drew her into his arms, he memorized the look of passion in her green eyes. "Would you repeat that last line?"

"I can't stand it," she said, breathless with desire as she twisted against him. "I ache for you, Max, deep in here," she said, guiding his hand to the moist triangle between her thighs.

"God, you're so ready," he murmured, stroking her. His heart thumped with excitement at the drenching evidence of her need. "So ready for me."

"Now, Max," she moaned.

"Yes, now." Slipping inside her, feeling her muscles tense around him, he thought he might black out from the pleasure. She arched upward, and he slid his arm under the small of her back. As he moved his hips forward she cried out. He withdrew and pressed forward again, heady with the knowledge of her response.

"Max, oh, Max . . ." She dug her fingers into his buttocks and arched her head back against the pillow.

He licked the perspiration from the hollow of her throat and kept on as her moans of ecstasy grew wilder. He wanted to give her the most shattering climax of her life. The pressure built for him, too, fueled by hours of thinking about her just as she was now, her body heaving under him without restraint, without shame. He gritted his teeth to keep from exploding before she did.

Then she gasped and trembled under him. He was still for a split second before driving home once more as her cries of praise rained around him and her body shook with the force of her response. Her abandon triggered his, and he thrust forward, unable to hold back the need to push into her again and again, to rub his sweat-slippery chest across her breasts and feel them tighten with the friction.

His vision blurred and the world shrank to encompass only Clare, who welcomed him with every stroke. He fit his mouth to hers and seemed to become her as, with one final thrust, he found completion. *I love you,* echoed through his numbed mind, but he kept his mouth pressed to hers and the words never escaped. *Someday,* he vowed, as the dizzy spinning slowly wound to a stop.

Slowly he lifted his head and gazed into her flushed face. "Worth waiting for," he whispered.

"Max, that was . . . spectacular."

"And that was with only about three hours of sleep for each of us. Just think what a good night's sleep would do."

"Does that mean you want to go to sleep now?" she asked, smiling a siren's smile.

"I didn't say that."

She reached up and stroked his cheek. "Max," she began gently, "you should probably know that this afternoon Durnberg told me all about your wife and the guy from California."

Max waited for the usual pain to hit, and eventually realized that it wasn't going to happen. This golden-haired woman had made it go away. "I'm not surprised Ham told you that," he said. "Ham loves the idea that I got dumped by a woman, especially one he once wanted for himself."

"I suspected as much. Max, this is really none of my business, but most people who go through a divorce have some financial difficulties."

"True." He tensed. He didn't want to talk about this. Not now.

"I've always considered you well-off, but tonight when I had some time alone to think about it, I wondered if losing this account could be a real problem for you, on top of the expense of divorce."

"And what if it would?" he asked quietly.

"I don't know." Anguish showed in her green gaze.

"Well, I do," he said, kissing her soundly. "It would make no difference at all. What have I been preaching here all along?"

"I know. 'Business is business.' But—"

"But nothing," he said, vowing to stick to his own creed. She mustn't throw this account away because she felt sorry for him. That would be the worst ending he could imagine to their story. He had to dispel her concern, even if it meant falsifying the truth a little. "Listen, Clare," he said, smiling at her. "You have nothing to worry about. I'll be fine, no matter what happens."

"Really?"

"Really."

"I guess Joel's hero worship isn't misplaced, after all," she murmured.

"Joel?"

"I didn't want to tell you before, but Joel wants to be just like you." She smiled. "Somehow that doesn't worry me anymore."

"Anymore?" He searched her expression. "But it did once?"

"Well, mostly because I'd like Joel to go to college, and when he found out that you hadn't, and he knew that we were a little short on funds..."

He saw the regret in her eyes. She hadn't meant to say so much. Now he knew that Clare needed the money from Durnberg's account to help pay for Joel's education. Damn. "If I keep the account I'll talk with him," Max said. "You're right. He should go to college. There are ways around the money problem."

"Max, I—"

"Never mind that now," he murmured, rubbing her lower lip with his thumb. "We don't have to think about anything until tomorrow."

"But—"

"Until tomorrow," he repeated softly, tasting her kiss-swollen lips as desire rose in him again.

12

WHEN CLARE AWOKE the bed was empty and the room silent. "Max?" she called, "are you there?" When no one answered she sat up and swung her legs over the edge of the bed. Max's note lay on the bedside table next to the box whose contents they'd put to good use the night before. Smiling, she picked up the piece of paper.

Meeting Ham at eight, the note said. *I understand you're scheduled at nine. This is not the personal part of this trip, Clare. This is the business part. Be tough.*

Fear made her clutch her stomach. The fun time was over. Today E. Hamilton Durnberg would make his decision between her program and Max's. She knew how much her agency needed the business, and what this account could mean to Joel's future. But if she won, what would happen between her and Max? He'd assured her that he'd be fine, but apprehension gripped her all the same.

Last night with Max had convinced her that she needed him in her life. He wasn't the logical person for her to love, but love was the only word that came to mind when she thought of Max. Their passion for each other was incredible, but her feelings went far beyond that.

She cherished his solid self-assurance and his kindness. His fantastic lovemaking aside, he'd also helped her through the maze of Durnberg's manipulations. Several times he could have allowed her to fall on her face, and he hadn't. He'd also come close to sacrificing his own welfare for her benefit.

The bedside phone rang and she picked it up eagerly. Perhaps he was calling her before he met with Durnberg. It was still five minutes until eight.

"I have a wakeup call for room twenty-four," an unfamiliar voice said.

Clare's shoulders sagged with disappointment. "Thank you." As she hung up the phone she thought about how Max must have arranged the wakeup call. He'd counted on an internal alarm to wake him in time for his appointment, so that she wouldn't be disturbed. Then he'd made certain that she wouldn't oversleep once he was gone.

A perfect example, she thought, of why she loved him. Some men brought flowers, but Max showered her with bouquets of thoughtfulness. The image of flowers reminded her of the satin daisies they'd fought about the night before and she smiled as she stretched her arms over her head. What a dope she'd been, and fortunately he'd put up with her until she'd come to her senses.

Maybe, she concluded, walking to the bathroom to start the shower, just maybe everything would be fine, as Max had said. He seemed unflappable, so perhaps even if she got the account he'd take it in stride. If anyone could do that, it would be Max. Then she could have it all—Max and success with her business.

As she showered and dressed for the meeting with Durnberg, Clare discovered that she loved her body more because Max loved it so well. The breasts that she had once thought too small were lovely this morning, because Max had praised them. She was glad for every bit of her five feet, eight and a half inches, because Max liked tall women with long legs. She almost skipped her customary coat of mascara because Max had said that her pale eyelashes made her look vulnerable and sexy.

By the time she swung open the door of her cottage and stepped into the warm Florida sunshine, she was ready for anything that E. Hamilton Durnberg dished out. If he took her program, fine. If he didn't, she'd look for other business just as lucrative. As long as her world had Max in it, she could do anything.

She found Durnberg sipping coffee at the same table where they'd all had dinner the first night of their stay. Beyond him the view looked as if it belonged between the pages of a slick vacation magazine. Sunlight scampered over the gentle waves and heightened the colors of the small sailboats frisking on the water. The sand below the restaurant was daubed with the bright towels and brown bodies of sunbathers, and seabirds swooped overhead.

Clare knew she'd hate to leave this spot. She and Max had never enjoyed a sunset over the Gulf together, or taken out one of the bright little sailboats just for fun. There hadn't been time to lie on the sand, or hunt for shells. Yet all the same, she'd enjoyed nearly every minute of her stay. Except for Durnberg's presence here, Sugar Sands had been a breathtaking experience.

"Well, Clare," Durnberg said, glancing up. "A white dress. Don't you look fresh and virginal this morning."

For one horrible moment she wondered if Max had told Durnberg everything, but then she dismissed the thought as being unworthy of her. Durnberg was only displaying his usual obnoxious behavior. "What a beautiful day," she said, ignoring his remark as a waiter pulled out a chair for her.

"Yes. I always think it should be raining when someone has to leave a place like this."

"That's one way of looking at it." Clare glanced at the breakfast menu and realized that she was starving. "Do you mind if I order something?"

"Not at all. Anything you want."

She ordered a lot—a dish of fruit, eggs, ham, blueberry muffins and coffee. Then she turned to Durnberg. "Are you having anything?"

"Just coffee." He signaled a waiter carrying a silver pot who came over immediately and filled both cups.

Clare had looked for signs of Max having been at the table, but if he'd eaten or had coffee, the dishes had been whisked away before she arrived. Well, he knew the answer to the big question. She wondered how long Durnberg would toy with her before he gave her the news, too. She couldn't believe how calm she felt. Her priorities now were elsewhere, and Durnberg couldn't manipulate her feelings anymore.

"So, Clare, did you sleep well?"

"Wonderfully, thank you." She blew the steam from her coffee and reflected that her answer was true. When she had slept, although not for long, she'd slept peacefully and well.

"I thought you might be up worrying about the outcome of this trip."

"No, Ham, I wasn't." She looked him in the eye. "I'd presented my case as best I could, and I couldn't do much more about it."

"I see." His perfect teeth flashed in a smile without warmth. "I told Max you were a tough customer. Cool as they come, I told him."

Clare glanced down at her lap. She couldn't show her amusement and possibly give everything away. She and

Max had been too successful in keeping their secret for her to ruin it now. "I'm serious about my business, that's all," she said, lifting her gaze when she felt in better control.

"I agree. That's why I've decided to give you the account for everything—life, health and both resorts."

Clare sat perfectly still and tried to absorb his words. For some reason she felt as if she had heard them spoken in a foreign language.

"You look a little shocked, Clare. Didn't you expect this?"

"I...I'm not sure what I expected, but after all, you've had coverage with Max for many years." She waited for elation to hit her. Instead all she could think of was Max, gazing down at her last night, telling her that he would be fine if he lost the account. But would he?

"Max is not meeting my needs, as you so aptly pointed out, Clare. Despite my long friendship with Max, I can't give him my business if he's not up to it. He's behind the times—no computer, no yearly review, and no Florida license. That was a nice touch, Clare, obtaining the license before you knew if it would do you any good."

"Thank you." Clare's order arrived and she wondered what on earth she'd been thinking of, to ask for all that food. Two eggs, sunny-side up as she'd specified, stared at her like accusing eyes. She felt the urge to defend the man she loved from Durnberg's stinging remarks. Yet she knew that doing so would reveal her emotions, her strong attachment to Max.

What she really wanted to do was leave the restaurant and find Max, so that she'd know first-hand how he'd taken the news. But she had business here, and she couldn't walk out on Durnberg now, after he'd just handed her this account.

She cleared her throat. "The Armstrong Agency's coverage of Flagstaff Fairways will continue until the renewal date of January fifteenth, of course, but I'll start the paperwork immediately for my agency to take over as of that date," she said. "Sugar Sands comes up for renewal on, let's see, March first?" She hadn't been hazy on that detail yesterday, but this morning she found concentration difficult.

"Yes, March first," Durnberg said, eyeing her speculatively.

"And the life and health insurance will have to be replaced gradually, as well, but we won't have to wait for renewal dates on those. I'll handle that with your accountant. I'll be in touch with him as soon as I return to Flagstaff."

"Fine. I've already called him and he'll be expecting you. Congratulations, Clare," he said, smiling again. "Now that it's over I can admit that I brought you along for the fun of it, to needle old Max, but you've performed like a real professional. Now mind you, I expect you to stay on your toes. No slacking off like old Max did."

"No, no, I won't."

"Clare, you can eat now. The hard part's over, and your food is getting cold."

"You know, Ham," she said, pushing back from the table, "I think the sporting thing to do is find Max and make sure there are no hard feelings. I do admire him, and I'd hate to think that we have to be enemies, just because—"

"He's not here."

She stared at him. "What?"

"After I told him my verdict he asked Santiago to drive him to the airport. I believe he's planning to catch a ten-o'clock plane."

"I don't understand. I thought we were flying back together about noon." She struggled to keep her emotions in check, but her panic increased. Gone? Max was gone?

"I suppose you'll be flying back alone."

Clare stared out the window at the sparkling water. If Max had left, then he wasn't fine, as he'd told her he would be. And if he wasn't fine, then they wouldn't be fine. She might as well face the bitter truth—by winning the account, she'd lost the man she loved.

"HEY, CLARE," Joel called from his spot on the carpeted floor of her office the following Saturday morning. "Can you read this?" He held up an open manila folder. "There's some unmentionable glop in the middle of the phone number."

"Oh, dear," Clare's mother fussed from her position beside Joel. "That must be another batch that got in with the pizza parlor garbage. I thought that I had all of those in my pile."

Clare sighed and stood up from her own twin piles of old, stained folders and rainbow-colored new ones. "Let me look," she said, bracing her hands against the small of her back and stretching before she walked over to where Joel sat with his allotment of folders. She took the one he handed her and studied the contents.

"What is it?" Joel asked.

"I'd say pepperoni, mushrooms and possibly anchovies, judging from the smell." She plopped down next to him on the floor.

Joel groaned. "I meant the number, Sis. And besides, it's sausage, not pepperoni."

Clare's mother craned her neck to look. "You're right, Joel. The pepperoni stains are round while sausage stains are more like a cluster of grapes, or maybe—"

Clare tossed the folder aside and buried her face in her hands. "I can't stand this."

"Pretty gross, isn't it?" Joel agreed. "If you think these folders look bad, you should have checked out Mom after she'd crawled around in the dumpster for half an hour. I came downstairs from studying for a test and smelled something putrid, and it was Mom."

Clare glanced at her mother. "I still can't believe you did that. I told you to get Joel. What if someone had seen you down in there, my own mother, pawing through garbage?"

"I wouldn't have claimed her," Joel volunteered cheerfully.

"I knew Joel had a test the next day," their mother said, bracing her shoulders as she offered her defense one more time. "It was very dark in the alley, and nobody saw me."

"Oh, Mom," Clare shook her head and despite herself, smiled at her mother. "You have gumption, I'll say that for you."

"And I got the folders," her mother added proudly.

"Yes, you sure did." Clare surveyed the floor of her office littered with piles of folders. The three of them had decided to spend the weekend copying the information from the old into the new, so that the stench from the old folders could be eliminated quickly.

"Another burst of air freshener, anyone?" Joel asked, holding up a spray can.

Clare wrinkled her nose. "I've had about all the Heavenly Lilac I can stand for a while. Joel, why don't you take a break and bring us each a submarine sandwich from the deli? It's almost noon."

Joel cocked his head to one side and grinned. "What? Nobody wants pizza?"

"Go," Clare ordered, throwing an empty file at him.

"What am I supposed to use for money?"

"Here." Clare got up and found her purse. "This should do it," she said, handing him a twenty. One advantage of having Durnberg's business had been a new freedom with money. Although she wouldn't be paid a commission for about two months, she could count on it and spend what she had accordingly.

"This should do it, all right, since the sandwiches are on sale for a buck-fifty," Joel said, pocketing the money. "Want a side order of caviar?"

Clare rolled her eyes. "Will you just get the sandwiches and stop with the comedy?"

"Right." He headed toward the door and turned back to grin at her. "It's great being rich."

"Yeah," Clare said, unenthusiastically. "Great."

When he'd left she sat down next to her piles of folders again. "Might as well do a few more before he comes back," she said with a sigh.

"Clare, I'm really sorry about this. You must be sick to death of your mother's meddling by now."

Clare glanced up and her heart wrenched at her mother's stricken expression. "Don't say that," she said, scooting over to put a comforting arm around her mother. "This was a great idea, and when we're done, the folders will look bright and cheery."

"But you seem so depressed, and I don't blame you, with all this copying, and the smell . . ."

Clare hesitated. "That's...that has nothing to do with it," she said finally.

"What do you mean? If I hadn't made this mess, you'd have every reason to be happy, now that you've beaten that Max Armstrong. But instead of celebrating we have to spend the weekend with these smelly files."

"Mom, I—" Clare hadn't planned on saying anything about Max, but she couldn't let her mother think that she'd caused her daughter's distress.

"Clare, what is it?" Her mother put her hand on Clare's knee. "Is something else wrong?"

Clare looked at her mother, and the tears she'd cried only in private welled in her eyes at her mother's sympathy.

"Clare, darling!" Her mother gathered her into her arms and Clare sobbed on her familiar shoulder. "Goodness, it'll be all right. There, there," her mother crooned, rocking Clare as if she were still a child. When the tears finally subsided she stroked her daughter's hair. "Want to tell me about it?" she asked softly.

"It's about Max," Clare began, and unraveled the entire story for her mother. By the end of it she was sitting up, dry-eyed and angry, fully expecting her mother to support her outrage. "Have you ever heard of anything more despicable in your life?" she asked.

Her mother spoke carefully. "From what you've said, I think you have strong feelings for this man," she ventured, rubbing the crease of her polyester slacks.

"So what?" Clare said, not even bothering to deny it. "He doesn't have strong feelings for me."

"He might," her mother said cautiously. "What if the loss of this business put him in a very bad financial position? A man like Max Armstrong wouldn't want to pursue a woman if he didn't have the resources to show her a good time."

"Mom, he said losing the business would be no problem. I think it's his pride that's hurt, and he can't bear to face someone who beat him in business, especially if that person is a woman younger than he is."

"So you're going to leave it at that?"

"Yes, I—I guess so."

Her mother shifted her weight on the carpet. "Tell me, Clare, if Max turned out to be nearly broke, would that matter to you?"

"Of course not! I care about the man, not his money."

"Then maybe you should at least let him know that," her mother said gently, "before you close the door on this relationship."

"Mom! I thought you didn't like Max Armstrong?"

"All I knew of him I'd learned from your father. What you've told me today, about how he helped you deal with Mr. Durnberg, even though you two were in competition, alters my thinking."

Clare smiled and nudged her mother. "And you've always been a champion of the underdog."

"Yes, I suppose that's true. From what you've told me, I feel a bit sorry for Max Armstrong, Clare, and I never thought I'd say that. He's lost his wife and boys, and now his biggest account. Not that I want you to give the business back. This money means a great deal to us, to Joel, especially, and besides, you worked hard for it. But Max deserves to know that you...don't care about his money or lack of it."

Clare gazed at her mother. "You think I should talk with him, don't you?"

"Yes, I do. The sooner the better, and in person. Face it, Clare, you really want to see him, don't you?"

Clare swallowed the lump in her throat. "Yeah," she said softly.

13

CLARE CHOSE Max's office as a safer place for their meeting than his home. She could appear on a pretense of business, a minor question about the Flagstaff Fairways coverage that he still held until January. If he was curt and uncooperative, she wouldn't stay. Any hint that her mother had been right, however, and Clare would pour out her heart.

She took a chance that he'd be there Monday morning. She'd left her mother in charge of her office, something she planned to do more often in the future. Belatedly Clare had realized that with Joel almost grown, her mother had become incredibly bored. She'd baked for the neighbors; she'd turned Clare's office into a jungle of greenery, and she'd splashed the files with color, all for something to do. Clare needed a secretary and would soon be able to afford one, so she'd decided to offer the job to her mother in January.

On Sunday Flagstaff had its first snow, and after her days in Florida, Clare had trouble adjusting to the need for scarves, gloves and boots. In a sense the extra clothes were appropriate, she thought, locking her car and trudging along the sloppy downtown sidewalk. In Florida she'd worn no armor, physical or psychological, against Max, but here, uncertain of her reception, she needed all the protection she could get.

Inside the hallway of the building she wiped her boots on the mat. After glancing at the stenciled numbers on the frosted pane of the door on her left, she figured out that Max's office must be at the end of the hall. She walked the length of it, pulling off her gloves as she went. The hallway smelled of seasoned wood, paste wax and a hint of cigar smoke that spoke of a solid permanence her shopping center office lacked. Clare began to understand why people kept their insurance with Max Armstrong.

The door to Max's office was unmistakable with its stenciled teddy bear logo and the slogan Clare knew by heart—The Armstrong Insurance Agency, Symbol of Security. She felt anything but secure as she wiped her damp palms on her coat. This would be even more difficult than she'd at first thought, and she'd thought it would be tough.

Through the door she could hear the muffled clicking of a typewriter. She'd forgotten about Max's secretary. Having someone else around as a buffer made her more courageous, and she opened the door.

A stunning redhead looked up from the policy she was typing and flipped off the power to the machine. "May I help you?"

"Yes, I—" Clare looked beyond her to the massive desk at the back of the room, where Max was talking on the telephone. He glanced at her and raised a hand in greeting. Just that, as if she were a distantly remembered acquaintance. Clare became icy with dread, but she couldn't turn back now. "I'd like to speak with Mr. Armstrong," she said and decided she should indicate more familiarity than that. "With Max," she added.

"Your name, please?"

Clare glanced back at the redhead and remembered that she must be Gloria, the woman Max had trained so well that one day soon she'd open her own agency.

Clare wondered if Max ever had been romantically interested in his secretary. It wouldn't be hard to believe. "I'm Clare Pemberton," she said.

"Oh, *Clare*," the secretary said, and her eyes widened. "I mean, um, if you'll have a seat," she added quickly, motioning to a chair against the wall, "I'm sure Max will be off the phone soon."

"Thank you." Clare sat down, and not wanting to look toward the back of the office where Max was, she glanced at the magazine table beside her. Copies of *Reader's Digest*, *People* and *Time* decorated the table, just as he'd said. Then she glanced across the room and felt as if she were seated in front of a rapt audience. The wall opposite her was filled with shelves lined with identical teddy bears, and all pairs of beady brown eyes were fixed on her. "I bet you wonder why I've called this meeting," she muttered under her breath.

"I beg your pardon?" Gloria asked. "Did you say something?"

"No, no, nothing," Clare said, taking off the wool scarf, which seemed to be strangling her, and unbuttoning her coat.

"I'm sure Max will be free in a moment," Gloria said, and fiddled with a paper clip on her desk.

"Fine." Clare thought the redhead appeared ill at ease and wondered how much Gloria knew about the Florida trip.

"Ah," Gloria said with obvious relief as they both heard Max hang up the telephone. "Max, Clare Pemberton is here to see you," she added unnecessarily, turning in her chair and glancing back at him.

"Hello, Clare." His expression was unreadable.

"Hello, Max." Clare stood up. "I—have a question about the Flagstaff Fairways coverage," she said, delivering her memorized line.

"Oh?" Max left his chair and walked around his desk to meet her.

She wanted to cry out with longing at the sight of him and fling herself into his arms. *Why did you leave like that?* she wanted to shout. Instead she swallowed hard and continued with her ploy. "I took a chance that you might be around this morning. It's just a small question."

"Gloria, would you please pull the file?" Max asked.

"Max, I just noticed." Gloria also stood up from her desk. "We're almost out of coffee for the coffee pot, so perhaps I should run to the store and pick up a can, if you can spare me for a few minutes."

Max frowned. "Gloria, don't feel that you have to—"

"I'll only be gone a few minutes, Max. And we need the coffee."

He cleared his throat. "All right."

Within seconds Gloria had grabbed her coat and purse and left the office.

"Max, she's acting very strange," Clare said nervously when Gloria was gone, "how much does she . . . ?"

"Not much," Max said. "Gloria's a good guesser, that's all." He gazed at her. "Why, did you think I'd plaster your reputation all over town or something?"

"No, of course not, but—"

"What did you want to know about the policy?" He started toward a file drawer. "I thought you already had all the information you needed."

"Not quite." It was sweet agony for her to simply watch him move and remember. He wore a charcoal Western suit today, similar in style to the one he'd had on the first day they'd met. Her gaze lovingly recorded the flex of his shoulders as he opened the file drawer and the way he cocked one knee against the cabinet while he searched for the right file.

His files, she noticed, were plain manila, not rainbow colored. She would have loved to tell him about the dumpster incident with her mother, and the latest news about Mrs. Bodiddle's dented car roof. But standing here in his office she was shy, unable to bring back the easy familiarity of their time in Florida.

"Here's the information," Max said, spreading out the file on Gloria's desk.

She prayed for courage. "Max, I didn't come here for that kind of information."

His glance was sharp. "What, then?"

"You said that the loss of the Durnberg account wouldn't affect our relationship, and yet once you'd lost it, you left without a word and haven't tried to contact me since." She took a deep breath. "I want to know why."

Pain flashed momentarily in his golden eyes before he glanced away and hid it from her. "You've heard about shipboard romances, haven't you?"

"Max, surely that's not all that—"

"Once the business was transacted and the suspense was gone, I realized that stress had brought us together in a fairy-tale environment, and that we'd be foolish to believe that we'd created something that would last in the real world."

"No!" She clutched the edge of Gloria's desk for support. "You can't demean what we had like that. I don't believe you care that little."

"It was fun while it lasted," he said with a small smile.

"Are you really that shallow, or are you afraid to let me know that you're in financial trouble? Because I don't care about that," she said, beginning to tremble.

Max looked directly at her. "Business is fine," he said. "Does this look like the office of a man about to go under?"

"Appearances can be deceiving."

"Clare." He leaned on Gloria's desk and gazed at her. "Go home and forget Florida. It was just one of those things."

"You're lying," she insisted through frozen lips. "You're lying because of some stupid male pride."

He shrugged. "Believe what you want."

"I will. And if you ever decide that love is more important than pride, give me a call."

"Goodbye, Clare."

She refused to tell him goodbye. She hadn't been given the opportunity in Florida and she wouldn't take it now. They weren't through, she and Max. She grabbed her purse and scarf and yanked open the door. She nearly ran Gloria over in the hallway as she left.

As Gloria entered the office she was shaking her head. "I don't think you used the time I gave you to good advantage, boss, unless she was running out to buy you a bouquet of flowers."

"I doubt if she's doing that," Max said and walked wearily back to his desk. Sending Clare away ranked right up there with giving up custody of his boys in the divorce, and he was exhausted.

Gloria followed, depositing her purchase on her desk and shedding her coat as she went. "She's beautiful, Max, and I could tell by the look in her eyes that she wants you."

"She thinks she does," Max muttered, plopping into his swivel chair. "She's wrong."

Gloria motioned to one of the two upholstered chairs positioned in front of his desk. "May I sit down?"

He smiled ruefully. "Do I have a choice?"

"No." Gloria took the closest chair and leaned her forearms on his desk. "I want to know why you ran that sweet girl out of here."

"You are one uppity woman," Max said, sighing. "Is this what happens when you have job security?"

"Yes. You don't need a secretary right now, anyway. You need a friend."

"Wrong." Max sighed. "I need money."

Gloria sat back and stared at him. "Is that what this is all about? I know everything's not rosy after losing Durnberg's business, but we're not—"

"Yes, we are," Max said quietly. "I have another big payment to Adele coming up, as part of the buy-out agreement for the business. I've gone over everything a million times, and without the Flagstaff Fairways renewal I can't make the payment. Right after Christmas I'm putting the house up for sale."

"Max, I'm sorry. I know you love the house."

He shook his head. "Not really, not anymore. But the boys do, and I always wanted to keep it for them, so that they'd have their same rooms to come home to when they visit. That's why I'll wait until after Christmas to put a sign on the lawn. Knowing that I was selling would spoil their holiday."

"What about Adele? Can't you ask her to wait for the money? Maybe something else will come along, and you won't have to sell."

"I tried that," Max said, running his hand over his face. "Believe it or not, I swallowed my pride long enough to ask her. She thinks I'm overly sentimental about the house and the boys' attachment to it. You see, Gloria, she doesn't want to believe that Tom and Brian care anything for their old home, because then she'd have to feel guilty for taking them away from it."

Gloria nodded. "Makes sense, although twisted sense. Damn, I don't understand why she has to have this money when it's bleeding you dry."

"I do." Max leaned his head back against his chair and closed his eyes. "I didn't give her a fair share of me when we were married, Gloria. She's still angry and trying to take in money what she missed in attention and love."

After a long silence Gloria spoke again. "Okay, I guess I understand that. You did work long hours sometimes, and I wondered how Adele put up with not having you home more."

"Eventually she didn't."

"But Max, what does this all have to do with Clare Pemberton? Are you just mad at her because she put you in this position?"

Max chuckled mirthlessly. "That would be a little hypocritical, don't you think? I'm the one who always said not to take business dealings personally."

"Then why did you send her out of here crying?"

"For her own good."

"Oh, sure, Max. She looked so much happier when she left than when she arrived."

Max opened his eyes and stared at the dots of the acoustical ceiling. They reminded him of the tiny breathing holes that crabs make in the white sand of the Gulf. "She will be happier in the long run," he said. "She's on her way up. She doesn't need to be dragged down by a middle-aged man with financial problems."

"Max, I could strangle you."

"Huh?" Surprised by the vehemence of Gloria's statement, he sat up. "Why?"

"You have made the decision for her, that's why. You've decided that you're a liability without giving her any chance to contradict you. She might not care a whit about your financial difficulties. She didn't impress me, in the few minutes I observed her, as being the kind of woman that judges a man by his bank balance."

"Gloria, you don't understand." He leaned forward. "She's young and impressionable. After the time we spent in Florida together she has stars in her eyes about me. She couldn't be expected to make a reasonable decision right now."

"Oh, so she's not very smart when her emotions are involved, but you, man of great experience, are?"

"That's right."

"Bull."

Max shook his head. "I wonder how many secretaries in the world get away with telling their bosses they're full of it."

"Only the redheads."

He smiled wryly. "Just my luck."

"Max, take my advice. Don't turn that young woman out into the cold. She could really light up your life."

"No question about it," Max said softly, remembering green eyes and laughing lips that pouted into the perfect shape for a kiss. "But I'd only cast a shadow over hers. No, Gloria, I can't take your advice. Clare is better off without me, whether she knows it now or not."

THE MEETING in Max's office was a setback for Clare, but she still clung to the belief that Max was embarrassed by his lack of money and didn't want her to know how much the loss of Durnberg's account had hurt him. If only she had concrete evidence that Max was in financial trouble then she could confront him and demand a truth that he couldn't deny.

In the month that followed she tried to imagine what sort of proof she could get. She drew a blank until Christmas morning, when Joel announced as they sat around the family Christmas tree that he was going over to Max's house to see Tom and Brian, who were home for the holidays. Clare had planned to spend the night at her mother's house anyway, but now she had even more reason. She wanted to be around when Joel came back from the Armstrong house. If Max was counting his pennies, Joel might be able to tell.

Reading a book by the multicolored lights of the Christmas tree, Clare waited up for Joel long after her mother had climbed the stairs to bed. Finally, near eleven, Joel's key turned in the lock and he came in, stamping the snow from his boots.

"Cold out there?" Clare asked.

"Nah, it's great," Joel said, taking off his knit cap and finger-combing his blond hair. "Tom and Brian and I went cross-country skiing in the moonlight. I used Max's skis."

His name, thrown so casually into the conversation, made Clare's heart leap with anxiety. "Did you talk with Max very much?"

"Oh, a little. He said to tell you hello, which I thought was pretty decent considering you took that big account away from him."

Hello, she thought. *Was that the only word he had to say to her?* "How is he—I mean, how are they doing?"

"Great!" Joel said. "I thought maybe things would be tight over there, but I guess losing that account was a little ripple in the great ocean of Max's life. He was the same as ever."

"Oh." Clare withdrew deeper into her easy chair, not wanting to face the consequences of what she was hearing. "So the boys had a good Christmas, then?" she asked, unable to leave the subject alone, fascinated with the horrible implications of a still-wealthy Max Armstrong.

"Super. Tom got a computer, which he'll need next year for college, and Brian got a stereo, with compact disk player no less, that really puts out the decibels. We rattled the windows a little until Max suggested we go skiing." Joel grinned and flopped to his stomach on the floor next to the tree. "I can't imagine why. Anyway, I'm glad he kicked us out, because skiing on the golf course with a new snow was terrific. We're going again tomorrow night."

Clare wanted to scream. So the world went on as usual, did it? Max indulged his children, ran his office, enjoyed his little life as if Florida had never happened, while she was miserable and felt as if a huge chunk had been cut out of her heart.

He didn't care about her. She'd been a convenient distraction, and perhaps if she hadn't committed the sin of taking away his business he'd continue to amuse himself with her, even now. But she'd demonstrated too much capability in his area of expertise. She probably made him feel a tad bit inadequate, she thought bitterly, and he'd dumped her. So much for her vision of a confident, self-assured man.

"Sis? Are you okay?"

Clare realized that the colors from the Christmas tree lights were all running together and when she touched her face her cheeks were damp. She turned away from Joel's concerned gaze. "Oh, you know what they say about the holidays. Everyone's more emotional this time of year. I got caught up in the nostalgia, I guess."

Joel was quiet for a moment. Finally he touched her knee. "Did something happen between you and Max in Florida that I don't know about?"

She sniffed and glanced at him. He always was too smart for his britches. He'd make a terrific insurance agent, or a terrific anything. Now that he was college-bound, thanks to Durnberg's account, Joel could be anything he wanted. "No, Joel," she said, taking a deep breath. "Absolutely nothing happened in Florida. Nothing at all."

14

A WEEK INTO THE MONTH of January Clare was summoned to Durnberg's office at Flagstaff Fairways to pick up a check for the liability coverage. Clare knew that the errand was unnecessary and that Durnberg's accountant could have dropped the check in the mail, but she curbed her irritation with a reminder that it was, after all, a very large check and the beginning of a whole new way of life for the Pemberton Agency.

She also listened with some relish when Durnberg told her of a condo damaged recently by a falling tree. Until January fifteenth, Max would be responsible for all claims, and he'd been unlucky enough to have this one only weeks before his coverage ran out. Clare considered the accident poetic justice and even allowed herself to laugh about it a little with Durnberg.

On the day appointed for her to pick up the check she left her mother in charge of the office without a qualm. Within a month her mother would be drawing a salary, and she'd be well worth it, Clare thought.

Clare's earlier mistake had been turning her mother loose on the office without careful training. Her mother had been like a curious boy scientist given the run of NASA, and she'd made an understandable mess of things. Now, with knowledge of the computer and comprehension of the filing system, Clare's mother was an invaluable asset to the agency.

As Clare drove through the entrance to Flagstaff Fairways she thought of Max and a familiar pain circled her heart and squeezed it tight. Angry though she was, she couldn't stamp out her longing for him, or rather for the Max she'd known in Florida. The Flagstaff Max she didn't seem to know at all.

Without examining her motives too closely, she decided to drive past his house on the way to Durnberg's office. The route took her out of her way by two blocks, but she couldn't resist getting just a little closer, even if it hurt to see the place where he lived in such splendor.

Half a block away she spotted the For Sale sign and swerved to the side of the road. *At last.* Shaking, she pressed her forehead to the steering wheel as thoughts raced through her fevered mind. He was in financial trouble, after all. He'd lied to her, but out of pride, not meanness. He hadn't wanted her to know, but selling a house without putting out a sign was difficult, and Max's secret was out to those who drove this street.

She understood it all, now, and wondered why she hadn't considered before the possibility that he'd put on one last extravaganza for his sons at Christmas time. Now Tom and Brian were gone, and the sign was up. Clare wanted to turn the car around and head straight for Max's office, but she'd promised Durnberg she'd arrive at exactly two, and it was almost that now.

She'd finish with him quickly, she decided, and drive to Max's office immediately afterward. Or she might call Max and suggest they have a drink together, she thought. His office might not be the ideal place for what she had to say, or what she intended to do, which was kiss him passionately and tell him to stop being such a dope.

Vibrant with hope, Clare swung into the clubhouse parking lot, got out of her car and hurried across the dry pavement. The resort's plows kept the streets and parking areas clear, but the fairways and greens held several inches of snow. Clare wondered if she could persuade Max to take her cross-country skiing in the moonlight, or anywhere in the moonlight, for that matter. The possibilities of what they might share if they could get past the stupid barrier of money gave her goosebumps.

She greeted Durnberg's secretary warmly. Before Christmas Clare had made good her promise to treat Beverly to a steak dinner. The evening had been pleasant, and Clare had wished that she'd been free to confide all of her problems with Max to this new-found friend. Yet she had feared that Beverly was too close to Durnberg and he might find out inadvertently that Clare hadn't been quite as icy as he'd imagined in Florida.

After Beverly told her Durnberg was expecting her, Clare walked quickly back to his office. She had more important things to do today than pick up checks, and she didn't want to waste any more time than necessary on this errand.

Durnberg smiled his predatory smile when she entered the office. His teeth seemed even whiter than usual against his deep Florida tan. "Ah, Clare," he said, rising and holding out his hand.

She took it and prepared herself for the bone-crushing handshake. Durnberg didn't disappoint her, and her hand throbbed as she sat down in the chair he indicated.

"Take off your coat," he suggested, "so we can chat awhile. How've you been? Did you have a nice holiday?"

Impatient with his desire to "chat," Clare nevertheless slipped her arms out of the sleeves of her tweed coat. "Fine," she said. "Did you?"

"Wonderful. I spent Christmas Day beating the pants off of the tennis pro at Sugar Sands."

Clare raised her eyebrows. "Sounds impressive." She wondered if he d picked the tennis pro because the pro's game wasn't quite up to his. She wanted to ask for the check so that she could leave, but apparently Durnberg had a different agenda.

"Yeah." Durnberg chuckled. "It was fun. You should have seen his face after the last game. He said maybe I should be instructing instead of him."

"Maybe you should." Clare swallowed the bitter taste that rose in her mouth as she listened to Durnberg's bragging. Even with all of his monetary success, he was an insecure man with a need to build himself up in front of people like her.

"Haven't got the time to teach tennis," Durnberg said, rolling a pen between his palms. "That's what I hire other people for."

"I suppose." She wondered how long she'd have to wait for her check.

"You seemed to get a kick out of my story about the condo accident," he said, a glint in his eyes.

Clare felt ashamed of the gloating she'd done, now that she knew the truth about Max's financial position. "I shouldn't have," she said. "I'll be in the hot seat next."

"Poor Max," Durnberg said. "Couldn't even get out from under before I had to file a sizable claim. We still haven't cleaned up all the details."

Clare felt a prickling sensation at the back of her neck. Surely Durnberg wouldn't pull a stunt like that. He wouldn't have brought her over here because he happened to be expecting Max. But he would, she knew, and she didn't even have to turn around when she heard footsteps behind her.

"Hello, there, Max," Durnberg said. "How nice that Clare hasn't left yet. Seems like old times, doesn't it?"

Clare turned slowly in her chair. Max looked like a gentleman cattle rancher in his Stetson and sheepskin coat. A furious gentleman rancher. His knuckles were white around the handle of his briefcase and his golden eyes had narrowed to dangerous slits. She was almost afraid for Durnberg. Almost.

Max's tone was deadly quiet. "You set this up on purpose, didn't you, Ham?"

Durnberg shrugged. "Not exactly. Your two appointments happened to collide, that's all. Clare had only planned to be here a minute, but the two of us got to talking, and suddenly it was time for your appointment."

"I don't believe you," Max said, with the same steady calm that spoke louder than a shouted accusation. "I believe that you're a bastard who manipulates people and their emotions for your own sick pleasure. You kept Clare here on purpose, to make her uncomfortable and to see me squirm. You've been doing a number on me for years, but Clare deserves better treatment. I warn you, if I hear of you abusing her in any way—"

"What? A threat?" Durnberg laughed nervously. "You must be kidding, Max."

"Try me."

"Max, Max, you've blown this out of proportion."

"Have I?" Max flexed the hand unencumbered by a briefcase. "I don't think so. Be careful, Ham. I may not be your agent anymore, but I'll be watching you. Thank God it will be from a distance." He turned on his heel and started out the door.

"Just a damn minute," Durnberg called imperiously. "You're not finished here. We have a claim to settle."

Max stopped briefly and looked back at Durnberg. "We'll handle everything by correspondence," he said, "and when I touch your letters, I'll remember to wear protective gloves. I wouldn't want any of your venom to rub off."

Durnberg's face twisted. "I'll get you, Max Armstrong. You can't talk that way to me. I'll see that you never sell another policy in this town."

"You can't touch me and you know it," Max replied. "I've done everything by the books, and I'll continue to do so until the fifteenth. The one thing I won't do, ever again, is kiss up to you. So take this job and shove it." Max turned his broad shoulders away from Durnberg and left the office. Clare wanted to jump up and cheer.

"He'll be sorry," Durnberg muttered as he rocked back and forth in his swivel chair. "He'll be damned sorry that he opened his mouth like that. I've got my ways. I'll notify the insurance commission. I'll smear his name so that—"

"No, you won't." Clare was standing even before she realized it. She should be frightened, she thought, but instead of fear she experienced a cold, hard certainty that she would stop Durnberg, no matter what the cost.

He glanced at her in astonishment. "What did you say?"

"You try anything with Max and I'll be a witness in his defense. I've seen how you operate and I've heard you threaten him just now." She felt cleansed, as if she'd plunged into a pool of clean, cold water.

"And who is this talking? My hired girl, who is about to make more money than she ever dreamed of if she keeps her nose clean?"

"I don't think my nose would be exactly clean," Clare said with a careful smile. "If you get my drift. And I mean it, Ham. You go after Max and you'll have to contend with me."

His lip curled and his eyes glittered like broken glass. "Isn't this touching, each of you wanting to protect the other? Maybe I've been wrong about you two and something did transpire in Florida."

"That is none of your business."

"Oh? Then let's talk about what is my business. I'm wondering if these policies will be yours, after all. No check has been transferred, now, has it?"

She'd expected this. He was giving her one more chance to grovel. Slowly she leaned down and picked up her coat and briefcase from the chair before she faced him. "Mr. Durnberg, gaining you as a client means a great deal to me and my family," she said and watched as he began to gloat. "They'll be disappointed if I lose this account," she added, while Durnberg smiled his evil smile. "But they'd never ask me to sell my soul for it." She left without a backward glance.

CLARE DROVE IMMEDIATELY to her office to notify her mother of what she'd done. Her mother, as Clare had known she would, supported her completely. "Now go find that man of yours," her mother had said, pushing her out the door.

And Clare tried. Gloria was extremely helpful, giving Clare phone numbers of friends and businesses where Max was likely to be. She made a steady circuit between his home and his office, but he didn't appear at either place. Finally, at a quarter to five, she decided to wait with Gloria at the office until closing time.

"Even when he's been out all day, he normally checks in about now to pick up his messages," Gloria said as they sat facing each other across her desk.

"That's the operative word—normally. This hasn't been what you'd call a normal day." Clare stiffened as footsteps approached down the hall, but they stopped and she heard the creak of another door. It hadn't been Max.

"No, not normal," Gloria agreed, covering her typewriter. "But this day's been coming for a long time. I wondered when Max would finally get sick of Durnberg's garbage and tell him off. I would have done it a long time ago."

"I think I know why he hasn't," Clare said. "He's always had the welfare of his wife and kids to think of." Emotion constricted her throat. "I doubt if his wife understood that he showed his love by taking all that Durnberg dished out, year after year, for her and his boys."

"I suppose you're right." Gloria gazed at her. "Well, now you're both rid of him. Now if we could just find that crazy boss of mine and knock some sense into his head . . ."

"Yeah, I know." Clare sighed. "Men. They always seem to have the wrong idea of why we love them. Max thinks he has to be a successful businessman to be worthy of me, when what I really cherish is his caring, his sense of humor, his warmth..." She glanced at the shelves of teddy bears. "Once I thought those bears were a clever gimmick, but now I think of them as the perfect symbol of Max. Did you ever read *Winnie-the-Pooh*?"

Gloria looked startled. "No, but not long ago, right before he left for Florida, Max asked me the same thing."

"He did?" Clare smiled.

"He did." Gloria leaned toward Clare. "Listen, it's obvious to me that you two are matching bookends and we have to get you together. Is there something we haven't thought of? If he doesn't show up in the next half hour, what will you do?"

"I don't know," Clare said. "Maybe I should camp out here with the teddy bears." She stared at the bears, who stared back at her. "Wait! I have an idea." She jumped up and pulled on her coat. "I have to run before my favorite toy store closes. If Max does come here before you leave, promise him anything if he'll stop by my apartment."

"Will do."

"If not, don't worry."

"Don't worry?" Gloria arched her eyebrows.

"Don't worry." Clare hurried out the door and down the hall.

By midnight, however, Clare had begun to worry, regardless of what she'd told Gloria. Where was Max? She couldn't believe that he'd been home, or she would have heard from him by now. If he wasn't home at this hour, where was he?

She paced through her one-bedroom apartment, located on the second floor of a twenty-unit complex.

Earlier in the evening she'd studied her surroundings and tried to imagine how Max would see them. He'd probably make the same comments he'd made about her office decor, she thought, because her apartment also had white walls and graphic-styled poster art hanging on them.

She'd attempted to create a spare, clean look in her furnishings. Using solid primary colors for enamel and slipcovers, she'd given the apartment a high-tech sophistication. Lately, though, she'd wondered if the place didn't need the softening effect of print fabrics and a ruffle or two. She'd considered replacing some of the bold posters with landscapes, and sanding the enamel from her end tables.

Yet she'd done none of these things, and she realized the futility of trying to redecorate in one evening. Besides, Max wasn't the sort of man to care about such surface appearances when deeper issues were at stake. At least, not the Max she knew. The Max she knew wouldn't be able to resist what she'd left on his doorstep, either. Clare glanced at the clock. Nearly one in the morning. Where was he?

She slumped down on her fire-engine-red couch and slipped off her shoes. With a sigh she leaned her head against the armrest and closed her eyes. She wouldn't sleep, she decided, but her eyes were so tired....

At the sound of soft knocking she leaped to her feet, instantly awake. The clock read almost two. Could it be Max? Heart pounding, she ran to the door and peered through the peephole. Then she grinned with relief. Reflected in the round lens of the peephole that made his Stetson look enormous was a disheveled Max holding a very large teddy bear. She flung open the door and he stepped inside, still holding the bear.

He gave her a lopsided smile. "So this is what you think of me, is it?"

She pressed her hands together in front of her and nodded. He was here, really here at last.

"You think I'm a sucker for Walt Disney movies and stories involving talking stuffed animals and cute teddy bears."

She nodded again.

"And you think that's our foundation for a lifelong commitment?"

She swallowed. "Yes."

"Well, you're wrong," he said, leaning the bear against the wall and tossing his hat on a chair.

Pain knifed through her. "Oh, Max, you—"

"Because we have much more than that," he said, stepping forward and enfolding her, pressing her against the leathery comfort of his sheepskin coat. "We have incredible, soul-shattering love."

As he kissed her, Clare began to cry, but he seemed to pay no attention as the salty tears mingled with their lips. He just held her close and kept on kissing her as if he'd never stop. His day-old beard prickled her chin, convincing her that he'd found the bear and headed directly for her door. Love! He loved her! And he still didn't know that she, too, had alienated Durnberg. He thought that she still had the account, and he wanted her anyway.

Clare's heart soared and she returned his passion, kiss for kiss. Before long they were tearing at each other's clothes and groping their way to her red couch. He pressed her back onto the cushions and finished unbuttoning her blouse as his tongue stroked the roof of her mouth. He unfastened her bra with one snap of his wrist and cupped her breast. She was gasping by the time he raised his head to gaze into her eyes.

"I've been going crazy without you," he murmured.

She arched her back as he rolled her nipple between his thumb and forefinger. "And here I thought maybe I only turned you on in Florida."

"You'd turn me on in any state in the Union, or any country in the world. I'd want to make love to you in outer space. Lord, Clare, I've been such a fool. Can you ever forgive me?"

"Only if you make love to me right this minute," she whispered, unzipping his pants.

"Clare, I raced over here without thinking. I didn't— oh, God—" He moaned as she slipped her hand beneath the elastic of his shorts and cupped the fullness of his need for her. "You might get pregnant, Clare."

"Does that matter?" she murmured, fondling him.

"Not to me. We'll be married as soon as you'll have me."

"I'd like to have you now," she said, smiling seductively. "And I'm assuming we'll want children. How else can we see all the Disney movies again?"

He gazed down at her. "I love you."

"And I love you." She moistened her lips with her tongue. "Seal the bargain, Max."

Fierce desire burned in his eyes as he pushed up her skirt. His hand slid along the silky length of her nylons to her garter belt. Without bothering to unsnap her nylons he reached for the delicate lace of her bikini panties. In a single motion he tore the flimsy material in two.

The sound of her underwear ripping drove her to a frenzy. She pushed his shorts past his hips and urged him forward. At last they would come together as a man and woman were meant to. The first velvet touch of him made her gasp. He hesitated, then thrust deep with a moan of ecstasy.

"Clare . . ." He spoke her name as if treasuring the single syllable like a perfect diamond. "Clare, my love, my life," he whispered, anchoring the diamond to a strong setting, to promises that would hold forever.

"I love you, Max," she said, breathless with the passionate tempo he set. "I . . . love . . . you—oh!" Without warning he'd brought her quickly to dizzying heights of desire. He paused and looked into her eyes. She felt that they were balanced at the top of a roller coaster, and the slightest movement would send them hurtling downward.

In the moment of silence their eyes said everything that words could not. Then Max surged forward, and they sped toward their destiny, their cries of jubilation echoing through the tiny apartment.

Afterward they slept until the chill of early morning tickled their partially unclothed bodies. They unwound themselves from each other and stumbled into Clare's bedroom, where they crawled drowsily into her bed and curled up together to sleep again until a pale winter sun touched their eyelids.

Clare awoke to find Max with his head propped on one arm as he watched her. "This is the first morning I've opened my eyes to find you still in bed with me," she said, smiling.

"It won't be the last."

She touched his cheek as she remembered the wonderful events that had taken place in the early hours of the morning. Now it was time for Max to know about Durnberg. "I hope you don't want to marry me for my money," she said.

He grinned. "Why else? I mean, look at the way I have to force myself to make love to you."

"Max, I'm serious. I told Durnberg off yesterday, too. He plans to cancel his agreement with me."

Max stared at her for a moment and finally began to laugh. "You crazy woman. You're crazier than I am. Don't you realize that you just threw away a small fortune?"

"Yep. Want to retract your proposal?"

He circled her waist with one arm and drew her close. "Not on your life, but I am curious. Why did you tell him off?"

"Because he threatened to smear your reputation and report you to the insurance commission on some trumped-up charge. I said I'd try to stop him if he did, any way I could."

He gazed at her lovingly. "Pretty brave."

"So were you yesterday. I knew when you took my part that you cared about me, but I still wasn't positive how much."

"Are you now?" He caressed her hip. "Because if you're the least bit unsure, I'll be glad to—"

"I'm sure, but that doesn't mean I wouldn't love to have you do whatever you'd be glad to do."

He kissed her lingeringly. "Isn't it silly? Here we are, poor as church mice, behaving as if we haven't a care in the world."

"Because we haven't. We—" Clare frowned as the telephone rang in the living room.

"Do you have to answer it?" Max asked, moving his hand up the inside of her thigh.

"Yes." Clare sighed and left the comfort of the bed. "It could be my mother, and she'd worry if I didn't answer at seven in the morning." She grabbed a robe from a hook on the back of the bedroom door and hurried to the telephone.

In a few minutes she was back. With a whoop she flung off the robe and leaped under the covers. "Where were we?"

"Right here," Max said, slipping his hand between her legs. "Was that your mother?"

"No." Clare chuckled and wiggled against him.

"Then who? Not that I really care at this moment."

"Durnberg."

Max's hand stilled. "Who?"

"You heard me. He was very humble and apologetic and said he'd very much like to have the coverage I offered him, after all. My guess is that he checked around yesterday afternoon, got some quotes, and didn't find anything to touch what I'd worked up. And he also said that he'd certainly rather have me as an agent than that hothead Max Armstrong."

"And what did you say?"

"I said I'd think it over and call him back later today."

Max threw back his head and laughed. "God, lady, you have guts."

"So, what do you think?"

"About what? He's your client."

"No, he's our client. Won't we combine our agencies when we're married?"

A slow smile spread across Max's face. "I suppose that's a logical step."

"I thought so. I even have a solution to your problem when Gloria leaves. I'm grooming my mother as a secretary, and I promise you she's very good."

"If she's anything like her daughter, she's exceptional."

"So, what do you think? Does the Armstrong-Pemberton Agency want E. Hamilton Durnberg or not?"

Max watched her with amusement. "I'll let you call this one. I'll handle the next big decision, but this one's yours."

"How about if we take him on, with some conditions?"

Max grinned. "I like this already."

"Condition number one, neither of us is required to play competitive games with him, ever, in order to keep the account."

"That's good."

Clare leaned her cheek on her hand and pursed her lips. "Condition number two, if we need to visit Sugar Sands Resort on business, we'll find our own accommodations elsewhere on Longboat Key."

"I like that, too."

"And condition number three, he's not ever to call us again at seven in the morning."

"Excellent." Max reached for her. "Congratulations, Clare. You've beaten Durnberg at his own game."

She nestled against him. "We have," she corrected, "by refusing to play. Isn't that ironic?"

"Fitting," Max said, running his hand over her hip. "Poor Ham. Such a game player, and he never understood the score."

Clare rubbed her cheek against Max's chest. "Sad, isn't it? He acts as if life is a tennis match where love equals nothing."

"When in fact," Max said, tipping her chin up for his kiss, "it's the exact opposite." His gaze was warm and golden with promise. "Thank you for helping me remember, Clare."

"Remember what?" she asked, knowing, yet wanting to hear him say the words.

Slowly his lips descended toward hers. "That love is everything," he murmured.

#257 DADDY, DARLING Glenda Sanders

Dory Karol and Scott Rowland had the perfect long-distance relationship—until Dory became pregnant. The prospect of parenthood should have brought them closer—both physically and emotionally. But Scott was a reluctant daddy, and it was up to Dory to make them a *loving* family....

#258 FACE TO FACE Julie Meyers

Griffon Falconer was terribly fond of his beard, and the sexy radio personality wasn't about to give it up. Yet that was exactly what Caiti Kelly was asking him to do. Of course, it was for charity.... In the end, when it came to a contest between his beloved beard and the charming persuasion of Caiti, one would be the winner by a close shave!

#259 STUCK ON YOU Kristine Rolofson

When wallpaper contractor Maggie McGuire was hired to redecorate Sam Winslow's mansion, she found his two small girls a delightful distraction. Their father, however, was just plain distracting! Maggie and Sam's immediate and undeniable attraction had all the makings of a sticky situation!

#260 THE HOME STRETCH Karen Percy

Dan Faraday was just the man for Cassie McLean. Pinetop's newest veterinarian loved horses, the small-town life . . . and Cassie. But Dan was only passing through. And Cassie had one rule for her man: he had to know how to stay put....

Your favorite stories with a brand-new look!!

HARLEQUIN
American Romance®

Beginning next month, the four American Romance titles will feature a new, contemporary and sophisticated cover design. As always, each story will be a terrific romance with mature characters and a realistic plot that is uniquely North American in flavor and appeal.

Watch your bookshelves for a **bold** look!

Harlequin American Romance

Romances that go one step farther...
American Romance

Realistic stories involving people you can relate to and care about.

Compelling relationships between the mature men and women of today's world.

Romances that capture the core of genuine emotions between a man and a woman.

Join us each month for four new titles wherever paperback books are sold.
Enter the world of American Romance.

Amro-1

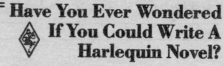